BEAR DANCER

BEAR DANCER

the story of a Ute girl

THELMA HATCH WYSS

MARGARET K. McELDERRY BOOKS ● NEW YORK LONDON TORONTO SYDNEY

For Lorin Marie

☺☺☺ ACKNOWLEDGMENT ☺☺☺

I am greatly appreciative of Venita K. Taveapont of Fort Duchesne, Utah, for reading this book in manuscript form. Ms. Taveapont is coordinator of the Ute Language Program of the Ute Tribe Education Division. She is the great-great-great-granddaughter of Elk Tooth Dress (Susan Johnson).

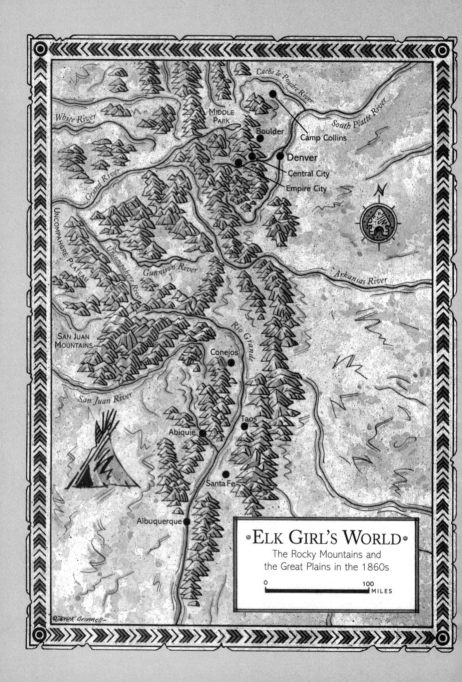

Cache le Poudre River

White River

South Platte River

Middle Park

Boulder
Camp Collins

Grand River

Denver
Central City
Empire City

Uncompahgre Plateau

Uncompahgre River

Gunnison River

Arkansas River

San Juan Mountains

Rio Grande

Conejos

San Juan River

Taos

Abiquie

Santa Fe

Albuquerque

ELK GIRL'S WORLD

The Rocky Mountains and
the Great Plains in the 1860s

0   100
MILES

©Derek Grinnell

Bear Dancer

1860–1861

◉◉◉ CHAPTER ONE ◉◉◉

At her first sight of the enemy, Elk Girl drew back in surprise. She reined in her pony, turning him around in a whirl of gray dust. She dropped low over his back and pressed her knees into his belly.

"Go, little pinto."

The pony, sensing Elk Girl's fear, raced back into the tall pines.

Elk Girl chided herself for being off guard. She had been riding across the high mountain, weaving through sun-dappled trees, and racing across blue lupine meadows far from camp, unaware of the enemy lurking in the shadows.

It had happened so quickly. She had burst from the trees into the sunlit clearing. And she had seen them across the meadow.

Two men on horseback. Their dark faces, streaked with yellow and white, leered from the shadows. Long black braids fell to their shoulders, wood bows and quivers hung at their sides, and long rifles lay across their saddles.

Arapahos. The ones with many tattoos. Dog Eaters.

When they saw Elk Girl, they raised their rifles into the air. Their sharp cries slashed through the silence of the meadow. "Ayee, ayee-ee!"

Now Elk Girl again urged her pony through the dense pines. The enemy was close. They had trespassed deep into the Shining Mountains.

At the beginning of time the Great Spirit had placed the high wall of the mountains between the Utes and the Arapahos. And for good reason: The Arapahos were to stay on the Plains and the Utes in the mountains.

Now this enemy had penetrated as far as the Uncompahgre Plateau, the mountain with the long, flat crest and craggy slopes. This enemy was bold indeed.

Looking for shelter, Elk Girl broke from the trees and raced her pony down the familiar trail toward camp. She knew the mountain. She had been born here. She had spent fifteen summers here. She knew the long trail that ran the crest, a three-day ride from one end to the other. She knew the red-rock canyons and deep crevices, jagged as forked lightning, that sliced down both sides of the mountain.

Elk Girl turned her pony from the trail and toward a red-rock gorge cut into the mountain. She nudged him forward, then gave him his lead. He dropped effortlessly down the ledges and stepped back onto a shelf in the sandstone wall.

Elk Girl slid from the pony's back and cupped her hand over his nose. "Quiet, little pinto," she whispered.

She heard the horsemen ride past the gorge and then return. She could hear them pacing back and forth along the rim, their horses snorting and blowing. They would not believe she had dropped from a cliff.

Elk Girl smiled. They could try to find an easy descent into the gorge, but they would not find one. Arapaho horses would not climb down a rock wall. Only mountain-bred horses could do that. Only small, tough, sure-footed ponies.

Elk Girl's pony nuzzled her and she wrapped her arms around his silky neck. She stroked his face, quieting him.

Elk Girl heard no further sounds from the rim. She wondered if the men were waiting still, holding the noses of *their* horses.

Perhaps they thought they were as clever as the Ute raider who had sneaked up on a sleeping Arapaho who was still holding the rope of his grazing horse. The Ute had cut the rope and disappeared with the horse back into the mountains, all before the Arapaho had awakened.

That Ute had been Guera Murah, her father. Chief Nevava had praised him for his bravery until his head swelled big as a thunderhead. Her mother had not liked such a big head in her tepee. One night she had leaned over and whispered into his ear, "Anyone who gets that close to an enemy should be clever enough to kill him."

Or perhaps the Arapaho warriors on the cliff were thinking that, in addition to a pinto pony, they would also catch a Ute slave girl.

A shower of pebbles rattled down the wall, bouncing off the ledge at Elk Girl's feet. The pony's ears shot up and he took a step forward. Elk Girl again cupped a hand over his nose.

She waited, then moved back against the wall. She touched the knife at her belt. She had always *thought* she was brave, as her father had been. But she had never faced the enemy—until today—and she did not know.

She heard no more sounds. She knew that, cunning as the Arapaho warriors might be, no enemy would wait long on top of a sunlit rock.

"We must go now," she whispered to her pony, "to the bottom."

As the pony worked his way down the gorge, Elk Girl wondered if a swift arrow might find her back. But she kept her eyes on the dark strip of pines below and did not look behind her.

At the bottom she turned. No one watched from the rim. Only a lone red-tailed hawk circled above in the cloudless blue sky.

"Now go, little pinto," Elk Girl said. She kicked her feet against his soft belly. "Go like the wind."

The sun was sliding down the sky when Elk Girl and her pony raced into camp. Dogs and children scattered out of her way, and women looked up from their meat-drying racks, startled.

Her mother ran up to her. "What is it, child?"

Elk Girl rode past her to the tepee of her brother. "Ouray, Ouray," she called. "Be quick."

The door flap flew open and Ouray stepped out.

"Arapahos," Elk Girl cried.

Before nightfall Ouray and his warriors were back in camp. Ouray hung two Arapaho scalps from a pole in front of his tepee. Then he squatted with his warriors to eat deer ribs around a small fire. Nearby, an old warrior began beating a drum: *tap, tap, tap, tap.*

The women moved from their tepees, stepping to the sound of the drum. Little taunting steps back and forth toward the scalp pole.

Elk Girl joined the women. But when she approached the scalp pole, she drew back in fear. Unlike these sneering women, she had faced the enemy. And she could not approach them even in death.

Her mother, Bird Track, danced up to the pole, shaking her fists. "Stay where you belong, Hateful Ones," she cried. "Stay where the Great Spirit put you."

Her daring friend Chipeta pulled at the long braids. "Are you sorry now that you came to steal our horses—"

Old Red Ant, fat and toothless, toppled down to her knees, laughing. "And our women?"

The women jeered and laughed. They hopped forward and back, forward and back. Crying *lululululu*.

Again Elk Girl stepped closer, moving her feet to the drumbeat. She stepped up to the scalp pole and reached out to touch the long braids twisting in the night breeze. But she could not. She spit on them.

"Maybe next time, Dog Eaters," she scoffed. "Maybe next time you will think before you come."

☺☺☺ CHAPTER TWO ☺☺☺

"Wake up, child. Your brother waits." Bird Track pulled back the rabbit-skin blanket covering Elk Girl.

It was still dark inside the tepee—and chilly, but Elk Girl jumped up quickly and dressed. Other Ute men did not take their sisters hunting with them, and she did not want to keep Ouray waiting.

Ouray was different. He had lived away from the mountains, down south in the village of Abiquie, in New Mexico. He knew

White Men and Spanish Men. He had much to tell his people, but they did not want to hear. What did it matter? they said. They were safe in the Shining Mountains.

But Elk Girl listened.

"Be quick, Elk Girl. Your brother is impatient."

Elk Girl reached for her bow and quiver of arrows and ran out into the gray light. She looked up at Ouray waiting on his horse. Round-faced Ouray, broad of shoulders, strong, sober, and cool-headed. He was not impatient at all.

They rode for a distance on the main trail, then turned into a grove of pines and quaking aspens. They tied their horses and crept through the trees to the edge of a small clearing. Behind the trees, downwind of a creek, they waited.

The deer came softly, stepping gingerly

through the dew-damp grass—two antlered bucks and three does with their young. They drank at the stream, looked up, and drank again.

Elk Girl set an arrow to her bow. Ouray put a folded aspen leaf to his mouth and blew gently.

The deer lifted their heads and turned their large ears. Again Ouray blew the faint cry of a fawn. A doe, searching with large eyes, stepped toward the sound.

"When it turns its head," Ouray whispered.

The doe hesitated, then turned. And Elk Girl let her arrow fly. The doe dropped in the tall grass. A second doe fell to Ouray's arrow.

Instantly the herd leaped into the air and bounded back into the woods, their black-tipped tails flashing.

Elk Girl knelt beside the deer and

watched its warm blood spill out onto the grass. She wondered about this gentle creature sent to her by the Great Spirit. With her knife she cut around the large, glassy eyes, the only part of the animal not to be used. Looking away, she tossed them into the trees.

On the return trip Ouray said, "You outsmarted the two Arapahos, Elk Tooth Dress." Ouray always called her by this name.

Elk Girl smiled.

"Always be wary of the Arapahos and the Cheyenne," Ouray said. "But, Elk Tooth Dress, remember always the real enemy, the one we can never defeat."

"The White Men?"

Ouray nodded. "There is no end to this enemy," he said. "No end to his warriors, no end to his guns."

"Utes will fight."

"And be destroyed," Ouray said sadly. "We must fight this enemy not with arrows but with words. I know, Elk Tooth Dress. I have seen."

Ouray had told her before about the power of the White Men against the Mexicans down in Santa Fe, and against the Pueblo Indians in Taos. He had seen, and he knew that there was no end to the White Enemy.

Today he told her about living at the Spanish hacienda with his brother, Quenche. When their mother had died, their father, Guera Murah, had taken them to the hacienda in Taos. He had whispered into their ears, "When you are older, my sons, return to your people."

Ouray and Quenche lived at the hacienda for many years, herding sheep, gathering firewood, and tending the horses. They spoke and dressed as the Spanish and worshipped as the Spanish. They were baptized

Catholics in a little adobe church at the Red River crossing.

Everyone thought they were Spanish. Even Quenche thought he was. But Ouray remembered the whispering, and when he was seventeen, he mounted a horse and rode north toward the Shining Mountains. Quenche did not remember and he would not leave.

Elk Girl smiled as she listened. She, too, was the child of Guera Murah, the "big thunderhead." Her mother was his second wife, the sharp-tongued Bird Track.

Elk Girl remembered the day Ouray returned to the Tabeguache Utes. "A little sister," Ouray had exclaimed when he first saw her. "A little sister in the mountains."

He had ridden through the towering San Juan Mountains to their winter camp on the north fork of the Gunnison River. He did not know that Ute scouts had watched him all the way. When he rode in during the second day of the Bear Dance, the camp was expecting him.

"I am Ouray," he announced. "The Arrow."

He made the Ute sign. With the fingers of his right hand he rubbed the back of his left hand twice, touched his black eyebrow, then made a circle on his right cheek.

"You are lucky you did not arrive with an arrow in your back," Chief Nevava said.

Elk Girl remembered how the young men had laughed. Because he had lived at the hacienda, Ouray could not ride, could not hunt, could not fight like a Ute. And because of that, no Ute girl would tug shyly at his sleeve.

Elk Girl looked at her brother now, confident and proud, a subchief of the Tabeguache. A great horseman, hunter, and warrior. But he seldom smiled. And he never spoke the name of the girl who had gone to the Great

Spirit during the last cold moon, leaving him with a squalling infant son.

"Do you believe what I say about the White Enemy, Elk Tooth Dress?" Ouray asked, riding close by Elk Girl's side.

"I believe you, but"—she hesitated—"most of the men do not. They say the sun of Taos was too hot on your head."

Ouray looked toward the horizon. "I know what they say. But if I do not tell them the things I have seen, will they trust me after?"

After the fences, is what Ouray meant. Even she wondered about this sober-faced brother who thought the White Men could make a fence around the entire Ute nation. Surely he knew the Great Spirit had already given them the Shining Mountains forever.

In the shade of a tall fir tree near her tepee, Elk Girl began butchering the deer carcasses, and Ouray rode out again to hunt with the warriors. Her mother joined her, and so did Chipeta, who cared for Ouray's young son.

"Do you have your words ready for the White Enemy when he comes over the mountains?" Elk Girl looked across a deer carcass at Chipeta. "The fighting words?"

Chipeta set aside her knife. "I will pull his long pale braids," she said. Her voice quavered. "And I will call him Pale Face."

Bird Track scoffed, "Foolish girl." She, too, had lived in Taos, and she knew. "The White Soldiers will line you up and point many guns at you. What will you say then, Chipeta?"

Chipeta smiled sweetly. "I will stand there bravely, Bird Track, just as you would, and call, 'Ouray, Ouray.'"

She reached over to Ouray's son in his cradle board, which was hanging from a low tree branch. "Little Paron," she crooned, gently swinging the cradle board. "Every-day you look more like your father."

The men returned from hunting just before dark. They pulled the deer carcasses from their horses and swung them to the ground, then sat around the cooking fire, eating and arguing. And reporting to Chief Nevava. Elk Girl took food to Ouray and sat near him, listening.

They had seen the White Enemy—five men at the bottom of the mountain digging rocks in a creek. They had lifted their bows to shoot, but Ouray had stopped them. He had talked to the White Men in their own language.

Chief Nevava glared at Ouray.

"I told them to take the gold rocks on their horses and leave," Ouray said. "I told them to go to the other side of the mountains to the place they call Denver."

A young warrior scoffed, "They mounted

their horses and rode into the trees. But as we rode away, they crept back to gather more rocks. I saw them."

"If we had killed them, they would not have crept back," another shouted. "When do Utes not kill intruders?"

Chief Nevava frowned.

Elk Girl trembled. Her heart ached for this brother of hers who knew so many things that no one else wanted to know. This brother who spoke four languages had told no one the fighting words.

Perhaps, Elk Girl thought, he did not know the words himself.

CHAPTER THREE

The Great Spirit dropped all good things from the sky: rain, blackberries, jackrabbits, pine nuts, and the black-tailed deer. And some things that the Tabeguache supposed were good but that they did not understand, like thunder and forked lightning.

But always the black-tailed deer.

Daily, Elk Girl hunted and butchered the deer. She cut the meat into thin strips and hung it over sagging buckskin lines and over tree branches that bent low with the weight of it.

"Enough now, Great Spirit." Elk Girl raised her eyes to the sky. "Enough black-tailed deer."

"Do not instruct the Great Spirit," Bird Track said, pressing strips of jerky into a painted rawhide parfleche. "Many times during the buckskin end of winter, I have wished for just one more parfleche filled with meat. But alas,"—she sighed wearily—"during those long cold moons when Mother Earth slumbers on, we boil the empty parfleches and eat them."

Elk Girl glanced over at Chipeta, who was also stuffing jerky into bags.

"Last night," Chipeta said, "when Ouray came to see little Paron, he said the same. 'Enough deer now.'" Chipeta smiled knowingly. "We will be moving down the mountain soon and then over to Middle Park."

"For the races?" Elk Girl asked.

Chipeta nodded. "For the races."

Bird Track shoved a stack of jerky inside a parfleche, then pushed it aside. She, too, needed a change from the black-tailed deer.

The small band moved down the steep Uncompahgre mountain, following a trail deeply rutted by tepee lodgepoles dragging behind ponies. Down through the towering, dark pines and the trembling aspens. Down through bright-green oak brush, and chokecherry shrubs heavy with white blossoms. Down through the stunted pinyon pines and the pungent, shaggy-barked junipers.

Finally they reached the grassland of the Gunnison River Valley, winter home of the Tabeguache Utes.

Elk Girl worked with her mother, digging pits for the dried deer meat in places they could find again when the ground was covered with snow. On top of each cache they built small fires and stirred the ashes to fool the hungry bears.

And to make certain, Elk Girl climbed high into the branches of a fir tree and built a platform of sticks where they could hide even more storage bags. Then she marked the tree with a strip of painted rawhide.

"I will fool the brown bear," she said. She did not intend to eat a boiled parfleche. Ever.

After two days the band moved on for the horse races. They followed the Gunnison River northwest until it met the swift Grand River. Then they followed the Grand northeast to the large mountain meadow called Middle Park.

Other Ute bands came down from the mountains: the White Rivers from the north and the Uintahs from the west. They trailed down from summer camps hidden deep in the mountains.

Tepees sprang up, white as chokecherry blossoms, on the high grassland.

After Elk Girl helped with her mother's tepee, she and Chipeta ran to the hot pools to join the other women. They bobbed up and down in the steaming water, holding hands so they would not lose each other in the thick, white steam.

They listened as old Skunk Eyes told the story about fooling the Spanish. "For two hundred years the Spanish down in Taos would not trade their horses with us," she said. "Against their law, they said. They rode the magical creatures while we walked. For two hundred years."

Elk Girl nudged Chipeta, suppressing a laugh. Could Skunk Eyes be two hundred years old?

"But one day," Skunk Eyes continued, "one day we stole one of the magical creatures, and another day we traded a slave child for one, and then—"

"And then we mountain-bred them," Chipeta said.

Elk Girl smiled to herself, thinking of her pinto pony, who had saved her from the Arapahos.

"And now," Skunk Eyes cried out, "we do not trade with the Spanish, nor with the Arapahos, nor with the Cheyenne. Now they fear us."

The old women cackled and turned over onto their backs, floating like brown logs around and around the steaming pool. Elk Girl and Chipeta, laughing, tried to keep out of their way.

Each afternoon Elk Girl, with Chipeta and little Paron, went to the horse races.

Men, women, and children raced. They rode bareback, kicking and yelling, as their ponies ran at full speed down a straight track. Two at a time raced until there were no more challengers.

"When will you race?" Chipeta asked. She bounced Paron on her hip.

"I will race the winner," Elk Girl said, "as he did." She looked over at a young man who sat straight and tall on his pony, spotted like hers. His long braids, wrapped in otter fur, hung down over his bare chest. He wore a blue bead in the center-part of his hair.

"His name is Spotted Tail," Chipeta whispered, "from the White Rivers. He has no challengers among the young warriors."

"I will have no challengers," Elk Girl said.

The next afternoon Elk Girl raced the champion, Gray Dove, who was on her black pony. The two girls rode at a slow trot to the starting line, then wheeled and started at a full jump. They kicked and yelled as their ponies raced down the track. The spotted pony won the race.

On the fifth day, as they again rode their ponies to the starting line, Gray Dove lifted a long willow stick. "Stay away from my whip," she snarled.

Both girls wheeled their ponies and the race began.

Elk Girl leaned low over her pony, clutching the braided rope around his neck. They rode as one.

Elk Girl was unaware of the black pony, of Gray Dove and her willow stick. She was unaware of the cheering crowd and of the wagered goods piled on each side of the track. She raced as if she were riding the wind on the high rim of the Uncompahgre.

The race was over too soon. The spotted pony crossed the finish line two horse lengths ahead of Gray Dove's pony.

Elk Girl's pony kept running, and she let him go where he wanted. He ran down to the river and slowed to a trot near a willow tree. The pony was snorting and blowing. And prancing.

Elk Girl slid from his back and wrapped her arms around his hot neck. He nuzzled against her.

She heard the sounds of another horse and looked up quickly.

Spotted Tail reined in his pony. "A very fast pony, your pinto," he said. "Like mine." His dark eyes were piercing. "I am Spotted Tail."

Elk Girl looked into his eyes. "I know your name," she said quietly.

Spotted Tail smiled, then turned his pony and raced off.

Sleep would not come to Elk Girl that night. She lay on her bed of willows, staring up through the smoke hole at the sky. Her head was swelling bigger and bigger, dancing around the tepee and up and out the smoke hole. Dancing upside down and around, twirling with the silvery stars.

"Stop singing," Bird Track moaned.

Had she been singing? Elk Girl slipped from her willow bed and darted outside. She slipped behind the quiet tepees into the trees to the horse corrals. She called softly. The herdsman jerked awake, waved in recognition, and fell back into his dreams.

The spotted pony moved through the herd and came to her. Of all the ponies, only he knew her call. Elk Girl put her arms around his neck and rubbed his long nose.

"I am too happy to sleep, little pinto," she whispered.

The pony whinnied softly, then blew. She wondered if he, too, had been dancing in the starry sky.

After the races the Tabeguache returned to their camp on the Gunnison River. They would race their magical ponies again in the springtime.

Elk Girl hunted small game with Ouray—jackrabbits and weasels—and from the skins she sewed clothing and blankets for Paron. Ouray hunted the great elk alone.

On a snow-bright day, Elk Girl and Chipeta took Paron, wrapped in his new furs, for a sleigh ride along the river.

"Like little Paron, I have no mother," Chipeta said as they pulled the sled behind them. "And no father."

Elk Girl knew that the Ute warriors had found Chipeta as a child; she had been wandering around a deserted Apache camp. They had brought her home, and she had become known as The Charitable One. She was light-skinned with a nose narrow and straight.

"You are my dearest friend," Elk Girl said.

The girls pulled Paron fast across the snow. They pulled him in circles, then dropped down beside the sled and laughed. After a while they returned to camp. Little Paron needed to rest before his father came to see him.

"Ouray comes every night. In his furs. Stomping like a bear," Chipeta said. "He scares Paron. He scares all of us."

"He is a great hunter," Elk Girl said, quickly defending her brother.

Chipeta nodded. "A great hunter indeed. And angry."

Ouray raged through the long winter, hunting during the day and, at times, all night. He spent many hours in council with Chief

Nevava, often leaving the chief's tepee in anger. He took solitary trips out of the Shining Mountains to the Plains. Spying on the enemy, Elk Girl suspected. But not on the Arapahos or the Cheyenne.

The White Enemy.

And after each heavy snowfall Ouray hunted elk. He waited patiently for the snow to force the large animals down the mountain. He watched for their wallows in the snow, and for the pits where they floundered in deeper snow. He pulled the butchered animals home on sleds made of their own hides.

After each hunt Ouray brought Elk Girl the prized teeth—two small bugler teeth from each elk, which she stitched onto her white doeskin dress. In return for the elk teeth, she sewed shirts and moccasins for her brother.

During the last winter moon, Bird Track

paced back and forth inside the tepee. She clutched her rawhide parfleche to her chest and whined, "Come, Elk Girl, and boil the empty parfleche."

"That time of hunger was long ago when you were a child," Elk Girl said softly. "We have much food now."

Bird Track only moaned louder.

After another of Ouray's elk hunts, Elk Girl roasted fresh ribs and served them to her mother. Bird Track ripped the meat from the bones, droplets of grease sliding down her chin. Still, she clutched the empty parfleche to her chest.

"We have much food," Elk Girl said again. She led her mother to her sleeping robes. "Ouray brings us meat."

One night during the long winter, Ouray became chief of all Ute people. He did not have the approval of Chief Nevava, but the Tabeguache warriors stood by his side. He stalked into Chief Nevava's tepee and made the announcement to the old chief himself.

Ouray was angry, brave, and feared.

And now he was chief.

CHAPTER FOUR

On an early gray-cloud morning of the spring moon, the bear rolled over.

In the camp on the Gunnison, Elk Girl woke to thunder clapping and rain whipping against the tepee. Jagged light flashed across the smoke hole. "Mother," she called softly, "do you hear?"

Bird Track sat up on her furs and grinned. "The bear rolls over," she said. "We will have food again. Come, Elk Girl. We must give homage to the bear."

Elk Girl ran outside, stretching her arms

to the sky while the silver rain splashed down over her.

All Utes would hear the thunder of the bear rolling over. They would fold their tepees and journey to the Gunnison. The White River Utes would come from the north, but not old Chief Nevava, who had fled there from Ouray. The White Rivers would come even though snow still lay on the shaded side of the trail. Spotted Tail would come on his fast pony.

"Elk Girl," her mother called. "Come. I will tell you the story of the bear."

"I know the story, Mother."

"And I will tell it to you again, my child."

Elk Girl sighed and went to her mother, but her thoughts were far to the north.

"Before you were born," Bird Track began, "and before I was born, a Ute hunter came upon a great brown bear still sleeping in his cave in the late springtime. The hunter knew this was too late for a bear to be sleeping, and if the bear did not wake soon, he might starve. So the man woke the bear.

"As a reward, the bear took the hunter to a place in the woods where all the bears were dancing to celebrate the end of winter. The bear told the man never to hunt bears. The bear said if the man would teach the Ute people the dance just as he had seen it, they would always be successful hunters.

"And it has always been so," Bird Track said. "This story you should always remember, Elk Girl."

"I will remember," Elk Girl said.

On the first full moon after the first thunder, the Bear Dance began.

Elk Girl rose before dawn, too excited to sleep longer, and pulled on her white doeskin dress with elk teeth stitched across the front.

She slipped into white quilled moccasins, then sat patiently waiting for her mother to wake. Only Bird Track's steady hand could draw the blood-red dye down the center-part of Elk Girl's hair straight enough to please her.

Elk Girl remembered dancing in the strong arms of her father when she was very young and, later, dancing with the older children outside the corral and peering at the adults through the fragrant juniper-bough fence.

And this year, when she was neither child nor adult, she would climb the juniper fence with Chipeta. They would look out of the corners of their eyes for the young warriors from the White River. She would look for Spotted Tail.

Elk Girl could wait no longer. She moved over to her mother's bed, slid her foot under the furs, and kicked.

Bird Track grumbled, but she sat up and painted the center-part of Elk Girl's hair. "Go to the dances with me this year," Bird Track said.

"Chipeta will be waiting for me."

"Go with me," her mother repeated.

Elk Girl sat with her mother inside the crowded dance corral. Cat Man stood in the center, swinging a long willow stick and shouting directions. "Men to the north and women to the south," he called.

Six strong men loomed over a rawhide-covered pit, a drum cave that would send thunder to all the caves where bears were still sleeping. It would wake them.

One man held a notched bone high in the air, ready to grind it against another bone to make the sound of the bear. The others held drum bones high above the covered pit, waiting to strike.

Then, at a signal from Cat Man, the drums and the chanting began. Like bears growling. Like coyotes barking. Like screeching eagles. Like thunder.

Again Cat Man signaled, and the women walked with shy little steps over to the north side to tug at the sleeves of their chosen partners.

Elk Girl stood on tiptoe to see over the crowd. "Look," she whispered, nudging her mother. "Chipeta is running straight toward Ouray."

"She is walking fast," Bird Track said.

"She is the first one there," Elk Girl exclaimed. "Of all the women, the first one. Cat Man is waving his willow stick at her."

Bird Track smiled, but Elk Girl did not understand. "Walking fast," Bird Track said again.

Cat Man directed the dancers to form two straight lines. Then, brandishing his willow stick, he sent all those not dancing out of the corral.

Outside, Bird Track joined her friends, chatting together. Elk Girl climbed the juniper fence and leaned over. She watched as the two lines moved back and forth, the men pawing the air like bears as they danced toward the women.

Elk Girl felt someone watching her, moving closer. She looked up and a little cry caught in her throat.

Spotted Tail.

She looked down quickly. Quiet. Breathless. And she did not move from her place on the fence until the dancing stopped for the afternoon feast. Then, when she peered around, she saw that Spotted Tail was no longer by her side. But she had known that anyway. She had sensed the moment when he slipped away.

On the second day of the Bear Dance, Elk Girl watched the dancing with her mother.

She looked out of the corner of her eye for Spotted Tail, but she did not find him.

Nor did she find him on the third day.

On that day some of the women dancers fell to the ground, exhausted. When this happened, Cat Man stopped the music and the dancing, and the medicine man from White River worked over the women with powders and feathers, and chased the evil out of their feet and up into the sky. Then the women stood in the line again and the dancing continued.

"Chipeta is still dancing," Elk Girl said to her mother at dusk. "I fear she may fall."

Bird Track smiled the same elusive smile. "Ouray will not let her fall."

On the fourth and last day, the dancing continued until sunset. By now the long straight lines wavered. Ouray and Chipeta stepped from the swaying rows and moved together to the slow beat of the drum.

Children danced with their parents. Old Cat Man discarded his willow stick and sought out his wife.

At sunset the dancers stopped to rest and feast, and when darkness came, the night dance began.

Bird Track was weary and she returned to her tepee. Elk Girl again climbed the juniper fence. During the feasting a large brush pile had been built in the center of the corral, taller than any man. As the drums thundered, Cat Man approached the brush, holding a torch above his head. With a loud yelp he tossed the torch into it. Red flames leaped into the dark sky, hissing.

In that instant two shaggy brown bears leaped into the corral, growling and pawing the air. The drums and chanting stopped. The dancers drew back against the fence. Children ran quickly to their parents.

Elk Girl gasped and clutched the juniper boughs. Even though she knew.

"They are only two hunters in bearskins," Spotted Tail said, suddenly appearing at her side. He placed his hand over hers.

The drums thundered. The chanting rose higher and higher. And the dancers moved as if in a dream around the leaping red fire.

The bears were awake now. All the bears in the Shining Mountains were awake and hungry and prowling for mates.

Elk Girl and Spotted Tail leaned against the spicy junipers and watched the last of the Bear Dance. Ouray and Chipeta wrapped their arms around each other, moving slower and slower. Then they slipped quietly into the whispering trees. Others slipped away. Soon there were no dancers in the corral, just the two shaggy bears swaying together in the dimming firelight.

Elk Girl's heart beat like many tiny drums. Next year, on the first day of the Bear Dance, when the musicians played the choosing song, she would run across the corral to Spotted Tail and tug on his sleeve. She would run right past old Cat Man waving his willow stick wildly in the air.

Walking fast. Walking fast.

CHAPTER FIVE

Elk Girl rode her pony at the side of Ouray. He rode a small mare, as black as a night with no moon. Her brother had asked her to ride with him along the Gunnison River. He was brooding.

"Little sister," he said, "Chief Nevava is still with the White River Utes. He tells them to fight the White Men because he does not know how to talk to them."

"Our father knew," Elk Girl said quietly.

Ouray nodded. "It was Nevava who called

our father home from Taos because he knew the ways of the White Men. Still, Nevava burned down the White Man's trading post on the riverbank. He thought the trader was cheating us because he could no longer sell our beaver pelts. Nevava did not understand that the White Men no longer wanted beaver top hats. They had changed to silk hats."

"Now they want golden rocks?" Elk Girl asked.

Ouray nodded again.

"But what am I to do?" Elk Girl asked. "I have never seen one of the White Men. When I do, I will be too frightened to speak."

"Chief Nevava's wife is old. She needs help with butchering and cooking. You could help her and talk to her. You would be respected as daughter of Guera Murah. And as my sister."

Elk Girl looked up quickly. "Go north to live with the White Rivers? Leave my mother, you, and Chipeta?" Her heart was pounding like a beating drum.

She thought of Spotted Tail at the Bear Dance. He was White River. Perhaps Ouray, too, was thinking of Spotted Tail.

"For the summer?" she asked hesitantly.

"For the summer," Ouray answered. "And later, with my help, you will become chief of the White River Utes."

Ouray reined in his pony and reached for Elk Girl's hand. "You and I, Elk Tooth Dress, were born not to the old way, nor to the new. We are caught in a time between. But the Great Spirit knows of us."

Elk Girl did not question Ouray. But she

wondered what the Great Spirit knew of Ouray, what the Great Spirit knew of Elk Tooth Dress.

Before returning to their high summer camp on the Uncompahgre Plateau, the Tabeguache again traveled up to Middle Park for horse racing. Ouray and Elk Girl rode in front of the procession, leading five swift black ponies as a gift for Old One, wife of Chief Nevava.

Old One was not at the races. She was too tired, Deer Leg Fur of the White Rivers said. But she was eagerly awaiting the arrival of Elk Girl and the ponies. Chief Nevava had also stayed at home. Elk Girl paid her respects to Deer Leg Fur and then rode her pony around the campground, looking.

She looked out of the corner of her eye at

first and then straight on. She looked every-where, calling *Spotted Tail, Spotted Tail,* loudly in her heart. She rode at a slow trot around the white tepees and then down to the racetracks. She raced her pony to the riverbank and through the willow trees.

When she could not find him, she sought out old Skunk Eyes, who was soaking in the hot pools.

"That one, whose name I do not remember," Skunk Eyes said, "is not at the races this spring. That one went to the prairie to hunt buffalo. That one broke his leg."

Elk Girl cried out.

"The hunters left that one behind," Skunk Eyes said. "That one is never coming back. That one is just a pile of bones on the prairie now."

The old woman faded into the gray steam,

and Elk Girl covered her face with her long hair and wept.

That night she could not sleep. She saw the face of Spotted Tail when her eyes were closed and when her eyes were open. At dawn, while her mother still slept, she slipped from her bed and went outside. She led her pony out of camp, then jumped on his back and kicked his sides. The pony broke into a run.

"Keep away, Chosen One," she cried. "I do not want to see you in my sleep. I do not want to see you in a whirlwind. I do not love you. I never loved you." The words were bitter and not the words of her heart. But the ghost must be told to go to the Great Spirit and not to follow her.

Elk Girl raced her pony into the foothills, through sagebrush and rabbitbrush up to the mountains. She followed a trail to the quaking aspens and the dark spruces, where flowers pushed through the crusted snow—pink primrose and yellow lily.

When the snow was too deep for the pony to go farther, she turned him around and rode slowly back down the trail. She stopped in a cluster of low pinyon pines and peeled off a piece of soft pine pitch from a branch. She touched it to her head.

Hesitantly, she reached for a larger piece and spread it down the center-part of her hair. No ghost would follow her now, not a wandering ghost with a broken leg and tears in his eyes.

The next day, Elk Girl hugged her mother. "I will return," she said, "at summer's end." Then she said good-bye to Ouray, Chipeta, and little Paron.

"My emissary," Ouray said, handing Elk Girl the ropes of the five ponies.

"But, Ouray—" Elk Girl felt frightened. She did not know the fighting words Ouray wanted her to say.

"Talk treaty," Ouray whispered. "Now Deer Leg Fur is waiting."

Chief Nevava had two tepees on the banks of the White River, one for himself and one for Old One, his wife. Elk Girl stopped in front of Old One's tepee.

"I am Elk Tooth Dress," she called. "Daughter of Guera Murah, sister of Ouray. I have come with five swift black ponies."

Old One lifted the door flap. She was stooped and her face was wrinkled. Her gray hair hung down to her shoulders. "I remember you," she said.

Elk Girl smiled. "I am here to help you. Where should I put my willow mat?"

Old One nodded toward the back of the tepee. "But first," she said, reaching for a water jug, "return this dead water."

It was an unnecessary chore, Elk Girl knew. Perhaps Old One was wary of Ouray's gift and did not want her help after all. Elk Girl dropped her mat near the door and took the water jug.

"I will return the dead water to the river," she said. "And tomorrow I will make a new water jug for you."

Old One opened her mouth, but no words came out. She lowered herself onto her willow backrest.

Rain fell during the night. Elk Girl heard voices outside. Old One was calling for the medicine man. Chief Nevava was ill.

Then Elk Girl heard the strong voice of the medicine man. "First Wife, can you not understand that Chief Nevava is sick? Stand outside as I ask. Ward off the evil spirits."

Elk Girl heard the whine of the medicine man's wife. "I do not want to stand in the rain tonight. Let Old One. She is awake."

Old One scurried into the dark tepee, mumbling and shaking her wet hair.

Elk Girl jumped from her mat and hurried outside. "I am awake," she said. "I will stand outside the tepee of Chief Nevava. I will ward off the evil spirits."

The medicine man frowned. "First Wife knows the medicine. She will stand outside."

But already First Wife was running back to her tepee.

"First Wife is sleepy," Elk Girl said.

"First Wife is lazy," the medicine man said. "But hold this and chant after me." He handed her a small bundle.

Elk Girl held the medicine bundle in the battering rain long into the night. Chanting and smiling. She would stand outside Chief Nevava's tepee all night, chanting whatever the medicine man told her, to ward off the evil spirits. She would do this for Ouray.

The next day the rain clouds drifted south over the mountains, and the sun returned to the White River Valley. Elk Girl rode her pony along the river, looking for the three-leaf sumac. With the twigs, she would make a water jug basket for Old One.

She rode far from camp, looking for the bushy plants. She turned from the river into a narrow canyon where patches of snow still spotted the north slopes. Sumac shrubs filled the shaded ravine.

She slid from her pony and stepped into the bushes. She cut slender branches until she could carry no more. Then, with her arms loaded, she stepped out from the bushes to call her pony. She looked up into the painted faces of three mounted warriors.

Cheyenne warriors.

She shrank back into the bushes and curled into a ball. Hoping the enemy had not seen her. Hoping she looked like a gray rock. Her heart pounded wildly, and she clutched the knife at her belt. She heard a horse moving into the sumac bushes. Then another.

Suddenly she was lifted up and pulled onto a horse. A warrior pressed his hand over her mouth, choking her, and he twisted the knife from her hand.

She struggled, gasping wildly for breath, but the man tightened his hold. She heard a wild neighing cry and saw her pony running toward her, a rawhide leash pulled tight around his neck. He reared and tossed his head.

Another warrior jerked the rope, pulling away her magical pony with wings of the eagle on his shoulders and claws of the bear on his hooves.

Cries of Cheyenne victory pierced the silence of the hot summer air. "Ah haih! Ah haih!"

TWO

For a Hat and a Looking Glass

1861–1863

The Cheyenne rode northeast, keeping close to the shelter of the mountains. At the mouth of a narrow canyon in a stand of quaking aspens, they joined another warrior guarding five ponies. A Ute scalp dangled from the bridle of his horse.

The men argued loudly, and Elk Girl knew the reason. She would slow down their flight from the mountains. Only one warrior was willing to be burdened with a captive on the long ride home. He was lean and swarthy, and his long black braids were twisted with rawhide.

He pointed to himself. "Twisted Hair!"

Elk Girl looked away.

Twisted Hair was in command. He bound her hands and motioned for her to mount her own pony. He sliced the air with his knife to show his intentions if she tried to escape. Then, holding the rope of her pony, he led his men forward.

Twisted Hair did not know the Shining Mountains, and he led his men into one box canyon after another, only to retreat. Elk Girl knew when he was lost and was secretly pleased. Even her pony knew and pricked up his ears.

They stopped only to water their horses and to indulge Twisted Hair whenever he spotted a lowly porcupine waddling across the trail. Each time, he sprang from his horse and clubbed the animal on its small head. Already three porcupines hung from his horse.

He is crazy, Elk Girl thought. During another sighting, she glanced at the other warriors. Their faces were scornful, but they jumped from their horses to help Twisted Hair chase the porcupine.

At dusk, at the end of still another box canyon, Twisted Hair turned suddenly and flashed his whip, striking Elk Girl across her shoulder. Fire shot through her body and blood rose above her dress. She gasped in pain. Sensing her need, her pony reared and kicked against the rope holding him.

Twisted Hair scowled and began the retreat down the canyon.

Ouray would come, Elk Girl told herself over and over. He would come and take revenge. He would carry her home to the Tabeguache and take away the blood and the pain. Perhaps even now, as Twisted Hair retreated from the canyon, he was waiting.

Ouray was not waiting.

On the following day she believed that Ouray would come then. Deer Leg Fur would ride down from the White River and alert him. Ouray would station his warriors at each pass leading down to the prairie. Ouray would be waiting for her.

Weary with pain, she slumped forward on her pony.

They were three days in the mountains before dropping down onto the stubby, brown foothills where the flat prairie rolled out before them. Twisted Hair seemed more confident now, although at the approach to each bluff he sent two of his men ahead to look out for enemies.

Ouray had told Elk Girl that the prairie was black with thundering herds of buffalo. But it was not as Ouray had said. Now the grassland was cluttered with the tents and white-top wagons of the White Men. And in between, small bands of Arapahos huddled in their camps.

Twisted Hair skirted the White Men's settlements but stopped for food and water at the camps of the Arapahos, who were friendly to the Cheyenne.

After another three days they approached the Cheyenne camp on the bank of the South Platte River. On a bluff outside camp they were met by a young scout.

The warriors repainted the stripes on their faces and the markings on their horses and followed the scout into camp. Elk Girl walked behind, a dry wind whipping against her.

An old camp crier strutted through the camp, calling out victory for the Cheyenne. Elk Girl already knew the tally: six Ute ponies, one Ute scalp, and one black-faced girl.

Twisted Hair and his warriors paraded behind the old crier. The Cheyenne cheered as they passed, and some followed the joyful procession. They admired the ponies and threw clods of dirt at Elk Girl.

Twisted Hair stopped, and for the first time since entering the camp, Elk Girl looked up. She saw before her a beautiful tepee, the color of the morning sky. Scattered across that sky were bright quilled stars. Elk Girl caught her breath at such beauty. Perhaps the person who lived within also had a soul of beauty.

"Emeeni!" Twisted Hair called. An old woman stepped out and lifted her arms in greeting.

Twisted Hair untied the five porcupines hanging from his horse and tossed them at her feet. He looked very pleased with himself. The woman clapped her hands, then reached up to embrace him.

Twisted Hair dismounted and pushed Elk Girl forward. "Ute," he said. He kicked Elk Girl behind her knees and she fell to the ground.

The woman smiled broadly.

Twisted Hair tied a leather rope to Elk Girl's ankle and tied the other end to a stake a short distance from the sky blue tepee. He untied her hands. Then he jumped astride his horse and continued parading through the camp.

Elk Girl struggled to her feet and moved toward the woman. But the woman threw a clod of dirt at her. She exclaimed noisily over the five porcupines and called her friends to come and admire them.

Elk Girl turned her head from the woman. "There is no beauty here," she whispered, and sank to the dusty ground.

All day under the fiery sun Elk Girl pulled porcupine quills, pricking her fingers on the sharp barbed ends. As the old woman directed, she sorted them according to size and placed them in small cases. When her fingers left marks of blood on the cases, the woman screamed at her.

Elk Girl welcomed the night, when cool breezes blew across the grassland. She curled up on the hard ground and listened to the night sounds—a pony grazing near the tepee, the soft lapping of the river, the distant yipping of coyotes. She listened for the low call of Ouray.

She believed it was for her own safety that he had not come. She remembered the talk around the campfires: If the Cheyenne suspected a captive was being followed, they would cut out her eyes. If she tried to escape, they would kill her.

Ouray would wait.

On a night when the moon was a full circle, Elk Girl heard the soft sound of footfalls behind the tepee. They stopped, moved closer, then stopped again.

Elk Girl's heart leaped. Ouray had come at last. She crawled the length of the leather rope and whispered, "I am here. Elk Tooth Dress."

A ragged yellow dog appeared around the side of the tepee, nose to the ground. He crept closer, following the scent of the porcupines.

A dog. Elk Girl stifled her cry of disappointment.

But she reached out to him with a piece of meat. He snatched it and backed away, gulping the food. He crept closer and lay down with his nose between his paws, watching her.

Elk Girl rubbed his head. "Stay, Lost Dog," she whispered. He whimpered and closed his eyes. Elk Girl curled up beside him and put her arms around his mangy yellow neck.

And wept.

CHAPTER SEVEN

"Do not try to escape while I am away." Quill Woman pushed a bowl of water toward Elk Girl. "You will pull quills for Emeeni until your fingers are worn off." She sneered at Elk Girl sitting in the dirt.

Elk Girl looked up but said nothing. She had been in the Cheyenne camp for two moons now, and she knew the old woman's words. But she spoke only Ute to the yellow dog.

Elk Girl knew Quill Woman was on her way to the quilling society. The day before, the camp crier had stopped outside the sky blue tepee, calling out the invitation: "To Emeeni, who has quilled thirty buffalo robes . . ."

In late summer the quilling society came to Quill Woman's tepee. For many days she prepared for the event with Pale Moon Face, wife of Twisted Hair, working at her side.

Elk Girl watched the two women as she worked with the quills. She placed the coarse and fine quills in separate piles according to length and discarded the broken ones. Her fingers were red and swollen from snipping off the barbed ends.

Quill Woman and Pale Moon Face removed the blue tepee cover and spread it out on the grass. They repainted designs that had faded and repaired quilled stars that had been torn loose by the winds. Then they wound it again around the lodgepole frame.

They gathered berries and plants for

dying the quills and collected their best tanned skins to decorate.

On the afternoon before the event, Twisted Hair came to the tepee waving a scrawny porcupine, its small head smashed and bloody. He presented it to his mother.

Quill Woman chuckled with delight and served her son a bowl of simmering stew from the pot reserved for her guests. After, she sat stroking the dead porcupine in her lap and admiring her sky blue tepee until it was too dark to see it anymore.

The next morning when Quill Woman threw back the door flap to greet the rising sun, Elk Girl walked toward her as far as the rope allowed. She spoke hesitantly. "Your tepee is the most beautiful one on the prairie. But"—she indicated the squalor around her—"your friends will also see this."

Quill Woman stepped back, startled. She squinted like a weak-sighted porcupine.

"Come, Ugly Ute Slave," she said. "I will take you to the river to wash away your smell. I will not let you offend my guests." She cut the rope from the stake and, gripping it in her hand, led the way down to the river. The yellow dog trotted behind.

Run, run, Elk Girl's heart cried. Surely she could outrun the old woman. Yet she stumbled as she walked, and when she reached the sandy riverbank, she crawled down to the water. Quill Woman held tight to the rope.

One day, Elk Girl vowed as she crawled out of the river, she would be strong again. She would run away from this place, back to the Shining Mountains. And—she smiled at the dog, shaking water all over Quill Woman—she would take the yellow dog with her.

At the tepee, Elk Girl turned to Quill Woman. "I will keep the fire burning and stir the dyes in the pots. And the stew."

Quill Woman gripped the knife at her belt. She let the rope fall. "Do not think of running, Ugly Ute Slave. There is no place on the prairie to hide from Twisted Hair. No place."

Elk Girl leaned over the cooking fire and stirred the pot of stew. Today she would stir the pots for Quill Woman. Tomorrow she would run.

When the water was hot in the dye pots, she added berries and plants from Quill Woman's collection—sunflower petals for the color of the sun, elderberries for lavender, and tall, slender larkspur for the pale blue of the morning sky.

Soon the guests arrived. Each woman carried tanned skins over her arm, and a buffalo bladder quill case. They went inside the beautiful tepee, chattering together.

When the sun was overhead, Quill Woman opened the door flap and pulled at

Elk Girl's rope. "Serve the stew," she ordered. "And serve me first."

Later in the afternoon she appeared again and said, "The prairie breeze is up." Together they rolled the tepee cover up high enough for the soft breeze to pass through and cool the women inside.

Again Elk Girl sat at the fire. But now as she stirred the pots, she watched the women quilling. They put the colored quills into their mouths and drew them between their teeth to flatten them. Talking all the time. And then quickly before the quills dried, they stitched them into patterns in the skins.

Elk Girl listened.

"I, who have quilled thirty buffalo robes," Quill Woman said in a commanding voice, "I, who have a warrior son and a Ute slave, have no buffalo hides to decorate. My son tells me there are no more buffalo." She drew a quill firmly between her teeth.

"My son does not tell me these things," Soft Cloud said, her voice rising above the others. "My belly tells me."

Shakes-Like-a-Chicken spoke. "My husband tells me the prairie is covered with buffalo—dead buffalo rotting in the sun. Soon my husband will kill the White Men and leave them to rot in the grass." Her fingers moved quickly over a buckskin shirt.

The women murmured.

"You know our chiefs will not allow our warriors to fight the White Men," Quill Woman said, "because of the treaty and the goods."

Shakes-Like-a-Chicken scoffed. "When our young warriors are angry because they cannot provide, what will the chiefs say then?"

"Fight the Utes," someone said. There was snickering.

Shakes-Like-a-Chicken pushed her sewing

aside. "So we can continue to line up for wormy flour and blankets with smallpox—"

"Enough." Quill Woman rose to her feet. "Do not speak evil of the chiefs in my tepee. The chiefs are wise—"

"They are foolish like you," Shakes-Like-a-Chicken cried. "You, with a warrior son who brings home no buffalo. Only porcupines and an ugly slave—"

She grabbed her sewing needle and ducked under the tepee cover. At the fire, she brushed against Elk Girl. "Black-faced Ute," she muttered.

The day was not the happy one that Quill Woman had planned. The rest of the afternoon, she sulked alone in her tepee.

Elk Girl and the yellow dog ate the remainder of the stew, and when night came, they slept in the tall prairie grass behind the sky blue tepee.

Before sunrise Elk Girl heard the old crier. The Cheyenne were to move south at once. White Soldiers were riding up the river, followed by a long line of white-top wagons.

The men rode swiftly out of camp to round up their horses, and the women folded their tepees and tied the lodgepoles behind packhorses.

They fled south over the bluffs in a long swaying line—first the elders, then the women and children with the packhorses, and then the horses. The young warriors rode back and forth along the line, keeping order.

Elk Girl rode Quill Woman's packhorse. She looked back, hoping to catch a glimpse of her own pony, and saw that Quill Woman and Pale Moon Face had left the line. They were riding their horses toward the east in the direction of the White Soldiers. Near the top of the bluff they slid from their horses and crawled through the tall grass.

Elk Girl followed on the packhorse. She, too, wanted to see the White Soldiers. Catching up to the women, she slid from the horse and crawled through the grass. She peered over the crest. In the distance she saw two lines of mounted White Soldiers and behind them a long line of wagons drawn by plodding beasts. Gray dust swirled above the wagons like rain clouds.

Quill Woman mumbled. "They say to our chiefs at Fort Laramie that they do not want our buffalo, they do not want our grassland. They just want to pass through to a place called California-Oregon."

"They speak lies," Pale Moon Face said.

A party of warriors rode up behind the women, stopped on top of the bluff, then swept down to meet the White Soldiers.

Pale Moon Face whispered, "Look. Twisted Hair goes to meet the White Soldiers."

There was a shout and the soldiers halted. Another shout and they lifted their rifles. Shots rang out. Five warriors fell from their horses. Twisted Hair and three other warriors turned and raced back up the bluff.

The women at Elk Girl's side began to wail piteously.

Elk Girl clutched the tall grass, staring at the White Soldiers. The real enemy, just as Ouray said.

The Cheyenne were confused. Soon the camp crier ran his horse down the ragged caravan, calling out, "They thought our warriors were Sioux. Our chief says White Soldiers cannot tell the difference between tribes. They thought our warriors were Sioux. The Sioux do not keep treaties as we do. We must not return the evil."

Quill Woman echoed the crier. "They thought we were Sioux. They don't know the difference. Our chief says—"

"Quiet, Mother," Pale Moon Face interrupted. "The chief does not know what to do. Next time Twisted Hair will shoot first."

Run, Elk Girl thought. *Now is the time. In this confusion.* She clutched the neck of the yellow dog to steady herself. But then she thought of the White Soldiers marching up the river and realized that running from the Cheyenne meant running alongside the White Enemy.

"This is not the time, after all," she whispered to the dog. "We must go south with the Cheyenne. For a time."

She looked around for the packhorse but could not see it. She ran to catch up with the caravan, the dog barking at her side. She ran past the women with the packhorses. She ran past Quill Woman, who waved her arms and screeched, "Come back, Ugly Ute Slave. Come back!" She ran until she reached the head of the caravan, far from the old woman.

She talked breathlessly to the yellow dog as she ran: The White Soldiers could appear over the rolling bluffs at any time. And if the White Soldiers could not tell the difference between Sioux and Cheyenne warriors, they for certain would not be able to tell the difference between an odious old Cheyenne woman and an ugly Ute slave.

CHAPTER EIGHT

Elk Girl and the yellow dog wandered with the Cheyenne between the South Platte River to the north and the Arkansas River to the south. They circled the White Men's cabins and avoided the Arapahos, who traded with the White Men and now had the dreaded smallpox. The warriors hunted for buffalo or antelope or prairie chickens. Anything to eat.

One day Twisted Hair brought home an antelope and two scrawny porcupines. The antelope was roasted, and the porcupines were admired and then handed to Elk Girl.

From a pointed horn of the antelope, Elk Girl formed a crude knife and cut the porcupine meat into strips and dried it over a rock. She made a pouch from the skin to hold the meat and carried it over her back.

But more often it was whiskey that Twisted Hair brought back from his forays, although the chiefs said trading for whiskey with the White Men was against the treaty.

At times the yellow dog brought home a prairie chicken or a mallard duck and dropped it at Elk Girl's feet. One morning he dragged in a porcupine by its tail. He whimpered piteously until Elk Girl noticed the quills in his nose and pulled them out. She ran to a creek for fresh willow bark and mud and mixed a poultice for his sore nose.

"We will take care of each other, Lost Dog," she whispered.

When the leaves of the cottonwoods began to turn yellow, the Cheyenne divided into smaller bands and straggled down to Fort Wise on the Arkansas River for their treaty goods.

Elk Girl stood between Quill Woman and Pale Moon Face in the long line of women. She lowered her head to avoid the blue eyes of the White Soldiers who handed out glass beads and red woolen blankets. She feared the soldiers could tell that she was not Cheyenne and, therefore, was not allowed the goods they passed out. She feared they would drag her from the line over to the high stone wall. And shoot her.

Quill Woman kicked her from behind. "Keep moving."

The White Soldiers could not tell after all, and Elk Girl returned with the women to their camp across the river.

Quill Woman told anyone who would listen

that the chief had told the white agent about the deaths of the young warriors who had been keeping the peace, and the soldiers had given additional glass beads to the mothers of the warriors. Even she, Quill Woman, had received extra beads just for witnessing the event. Now, because she had forced her Ute slave to stand in line, she had more beads than any woman in camp. And an extra red blanket.

All day Quill Woman bragged about the glass beads. But that night when Elk Girl lay awake looking at the stars, she saw Quill Woman slip away to the river and hurl the beads into the water.

Elk Girl heard her mutter as she returned, "Never, never will I stitch the White Men's beads. Not in my tepee. Not I, Emeeni, who have quilled thirty buffalo robes . . ."

The following day Twisted Hair came to the tepee with sacks of flour, beans, and coffee, which he divided between Quill Woman and Pale Moon Face. He also brought a bolt of Turkey-red calico and an iron cooking pot, which he did not know how to divide.

In the end Quill Woman wrapped the calico around her sky blue tepee, and Pale Moon Face took home the iron pot to cook a stew for her husband. They used the sacks of treaty goods to sit on.

Everyone feasted well from the new cooking pots. The warriors, feeling good, painted their faces and left for the mountains to raid the Utes.

Before Twisted Hair left, Quill Woman told him to fasten a new rope around Elk Girl's ankle. She would allow her slave to sleep inside the tepee now, but she would clutch the end of the rope. "In the event"— she scolded—"you think of following the warriors to the mountains."

Quill Woman did not remove the rope until weeks later, when the Cheyenne were far north of the Arkansas River and the howling winds had blown the Turkey-red calico from her tepee out over the frozen prairie. She was weak from hunger, and she sat up in her sleeping robes and cried, "Give me the meat you carry on your back."

Elk Girl, lying across from her, replied, "Cut the rope from my ankle."

It was the time of the hard-face moon. Elk Girl added strips of the dried porcupine meat to the cooking pot. And she learned to make a dough from the treaty flour, which she dropped into the hot stew.

Along with the goods from Fort Wise, the White Men's smallpox had traveled home with the Cheyenne. Quill Woman said the pox spirit was hidden in the red blankets and threw hers into the river. She sneered at Elk Girl's suggestion that they move the tepee to higher ground away from the sickness in camp.

But as the disease crept from tepee to tepee, she cried, "The pox spirit moves in a circle. I will fool it." And they moved the tepee.

Isolated from her friends, Quill Woman became restless. She said to Elk Girl, "I will teach you the quillwork. It is a great honor for you to learn from Emeeni." She gave Elk Girl two antelope skins to make herself a dress and a pair of moccasins.

Elk Girl accepted the skins grudgingly, vowing to herself that she would not learn to quill. She wanted nothing from the old woman except her freedom.

Nevertheless, Quill Woman laid out a buckskin and her collection of dyed quills and began instructing. "These quills are longer and finer than those of my friends," she said. "My son brings me porcupines from the mountains."

Elk Girl shuddered, remembering.

The cold, gray days passed slowly, and on a night when the wind lashed against the tepee, Elk Girl sat stitching with Quill Woman beside a small fire. Quill Woman turned to her and said, "You are Cheyenne now, like Emeeni." She smiled broadly and her small dark eyes sparkled in the firelight.

Elk Girl looked down at the quillwork in her hands. It seemed like a long time since she had hated Quill Woman and a long time since she had dreamed of her home in the mountains as she lay in her bed. She no longer listened for the sound of footfalls during the night.

Perhaps she had no heart left for caring, just an empty place inside her. She reached out to stroke the dog lying at her side. She cared for the dog.

Quill Woman pushed a log into the

dimming fire. She peered again into Elk Girl's face. "You will forget Ute now?"

The wind whistled down the smoke hole, and Elk Girl pretended she had not heard the old woman. When Quill Woman looked away, Elk Girl whispered into the fire, "Never. Never forget Ute."

When the snow began to melt along the South Platte River, the Cheyenne women flocked like brown birds over the prairie, digging for roots.

Elk Girl was working at the side of Pale Moon Face when the spring rain fell from a sunny sky. The women dropped their digging sticks and lifted their arms, calling happily to one another as the rain splashed down upon their heads.

For an instant Elk Girl thought the voices in the rain were those of her mother and Chipeta. But just as quickly she knew it was not so. Wearily she left the chattering women and walked back to the sky blue tepee, carrying a basket of wild turnips.

That night rain came again and thunder rolled across the dark sky. The bear rolled in his cave.

In her sleep Elk Girl danced, her arms linked to a long line of women swaying to the beat of drums. The spicy scent of juniper boughs made her dizzy. She sat up, trembling.

She glanced across at Quill Woman buried in her furs. She dressed quickly. She thrust a water jug into her pouch and secured a horn knife at her belt.

The yellow dog woke and looked at her, wagging his tail. Elk Girl reached down and rubbed his scruffy neck. "Come, Lost Dog," she whispered.

Together they slipped from the sky blue tepee into the falling rain.

◉ ◉ ◉

As Quill Woman had told her, there was no place on the prairie to hide from Twisted Hair. Two days later, he caught up with her. He beat her with his whip, and when the yellow dog leaped at him, he turned his whip on the dog.

On the return trip they met a band of Arapahos in search of buffalo. Twisted Hair traded Elk Girl to a pock-faced warrior with a long nose for a sack of wormy treaty flour. He traded the yellow dog for another sack.

"This is a no-good Ute," Twisted Hair said in gestures to the Arapaho. "But good slave. Good slave."

He tossed the two sacks of flour onto the back of his horse and rode away, chuckling over his good bargain.

CHAPTER NINE

The Arapaho soon agreed that Elk Girl was a no-good Ute. Each night she ran away with her yellow dog toward the mountains. Soon he grew tired of chasing after her. He tied a braided rope to her ankle and turned her over to his wife.

"Magpie, wife of Long Nose," the woman said, pointing to herself. Then she pointed to Elk Girl. "Magpie's slave." She grinned and led Elk Girl to a pile of deer hides to be turned into buckskins and furs.

Elk Girl knew she was now the Arapaho

woman's slave. On her knees Elk Girl leaned over a hide staked to the ground. She pulled a scraper down its length, removing the hair. Over and over again she scraped in short even strokes, taking care not to tear the skin.

The work was tedious, but she knew it well and did not mind it. As she worked, she talked to the yellow dog frisking around her.

She vowed she would not be Magpie's slave for long. She would please her for a time, but one day when Magpie no longer guarded her, she and the dog would slip away.

As soon as Elk Girl finished one hide, Magpie brought another. And then another. Magpie sat in the shade of a cottonwood tree, holding the end of Elk Girl's rope and talking to friends who passed by.

Elk Girl observed the women as she worked over the hides. They were tall and stately, as graceful in their movements as deer in a mountain meadow. They had blue circles tattooed on their foreheads.

After the hides were scraped, Elk Girl began the tanning process. She rubbed a paste of animal fat and brains over each hide to soften it, then soaked it in water, wrung it out, and staked it again to the ground.

She rubbed and pulled and kneaded while Magpie's friends gathered in the shade of the cottonwood tree, watching her. They turned their heads whenever she glanced up. Elk Girl smiled to herself. The women knew they could not make buckskin as soft and durable as Ute women did. They did not care to work that hard.

Magpie examined the finished buckskins, the color of the golden sand on the river-bank. Elk Girl could tell she was pleased. But she wanted more. With gestures and simple words she instructed Elk Girl to make a shirt and leggings for Long Nose. He was going on a hunting trip. Elk Girl was to work inside the tepee while he was away.

For many days inside the tepee Elk Girl worked on the shirt and leggings. She also made a pair of moccasins for Long Nose and decorated them with quills.

When she finished, she stepped outside to show Magpie. Perhaps now, she thought, she could go down to the creek to bathe. Her heart lifted as she saw the yellow dog bounding toward her through the tall grass. She and the dog would go together to the creek.

Magpie frowned at the clothing, although her eyes revealed her delight. She motioned for Elk Girl to go back inside the tepee.

Elk Girl was cutting out a pair of moccasins for Magpie when she heard the hunters return. The camp was noisy with celebration. She lifted the door flap and hurried outside. Surely Magpie would want help with a meal for Long Nose. But first, she must find the yellow dog.

She called, but he did not come. She stooped to pick up her ankle rope, and saw Magpie at the cooking fire. Stirring and grinning.

That night under a thin silver moon, Elk Girl sat tied to a stake near the cotton-wood tree. She watched Long Nose and Magpie feasting together near the fire. Long Nose sat erect and turned his head to one side so Magpie could admire his long, curved nose and his sleek black braids. He knew he was handsome even with his pockmarks.

He was pleased with the buckskin cloth-ing, Elk Girl could tell. He was also pleased with the yellow dog his wife had served. He rubbed his belly.

Magpie grinned at her husband and then

over her shoulder at Elk Girl, who was sitting alone.

"Great Spirit," Elk Girl cried into the darkness. "He was only a yellow dog. A lost yellow dog."

She wept long into the night.

Snow fell, and the Arapahos moved to their winter campground near the foothills of Boulder Creek. The White Men were there, living in log cabins.

The angry young warriors prepared to defend their territory but were suppressed by their chief.

Like the Cheyenne chiefs, the Arapaho chief also wanted to avoid conflict. He, too, had been at Fort Laramie. If they kept the treaty, he told his people, perhaps the White Men would go away in the spring.

The Arapahos camped on the outskirts of town.

When the mountain passes were deep with snow, Magpie cut the rope from Elk Girl's ankle. She told Long Nose she was tired of guarding the slave, although the beautiful tanned buckskins were worth every watchful minute. But now she wanted to curl up in warm buffalo robes for the winter.

Elk Girl understood.

"You, Black Ute," Magpie said, pointing her finger. "You keep the fire burning and the pot simmering. If you try to escape, Long Nose will trade you to a White Man, who will lock you inside a wooden tepee." She chuckled. "And you will never see the blue sky again."

She sank deep into a pile of buffalo robes.

Snow still covered the ground when the Arapahos moved again. They traveled north-east to the wide South Platte River, away from the White Men.

No, Elk Girl thought, *not away from the mountains.* She watched anxiously as she helped Magpie roll the tepee and load the packhorse. She had to escape. As soon as the band started moving, she would drop behind. And run.

Suddenly Long Nose appeared. He pushed her to the ground and tied a leather rope to her ankle and the other end to Magpie's belt. Then he rode off to round up his horses.

Elk Girl sat on the frozen ground, dizzy with pain. At her side Magpie jerked the rope, impatient to be moving.

Elk Girl stood and moved closer to Magpie. "Give me the rope, Magpie."

Magpie understood, but she jerked the rope, and grinned.

"Then you must run with me," Elk Girl said. And she ran, dragging Magpie over the ragged ground. She did not go far before Long Nose came to his wife's rescue.

Magpie was scratched and her beautiful doeskin dress was torn and muddy. "Trade the black Ute," she cried.

In camp on the Platte riverbank, Long Nose tied Elk Girl to a cottonwood tree. Then he gathered several young warriors and rode swiftly out of camp.

It was daybreak when he returned. He pulled Elk Girl to her feet. "Get up, Black Ute."

Elk Girl looked up and saw a blue-eyed White Man sitting on a tall gray horse. He wore buckskin and a wide-brimmed hat. His curly hair was tied at the back of his neck. Under one arm he clutched a board that shimmered in the firelight. He kept glancing at it, as if surprised to be holding it.

Elk Girl pulled back, trembling with fear. This was the real enemy.

Long Nose pushed Elk Girl forward.

"Swap, swap." He pointed to the man's hat and the shining board.

The White Man looked down at Elk Girl, his blue eyes sad. He slowly shook his head.

Long Nose grabbed for the board. "Swap magic looking glass. Swap big hat." He pointed to Elk Girl. "Swap for Ute girl."

The White Man spoke loudly and shook his head again.

Long Nose understood the answer. He began yelping. The other warriors joined in.

The White Man touched his knees to his horse and rode quickly out of camp, still clutching the looking glass under his arm.

In a rage Long Nose lashed out at Elk Girl with his whip. She turned from him, and he beat her across her back and legs until blood trickled down her body. She ran, but she could not break through the circle of jeering warriors, who pushed her back.

Yelping loudly, Long Nose seized her long hair and, with his knife, sheared her hair from her head. It fell about her in black waves.

Covering her shorn head with her arms, Elk Girl sank to the ground. She cried in despair, "Great Spirit, do you know of me: Elk Tooth Dress? Do you know of me?"

All morning the Arapahos gathered dry brush from the riverbank and piled it high in the center of camp. At dusk Long Nose set a torch to it. The fire hissed and crackled in the darkening sky.

The old men squatted around the fire beating drums and chanting. The young warriors danced to the hypnotic beat. Faster and faster. Louder and louder.

Frightened, Elk Girl watched from the cottonwood tree where Long Nose had tied her.

Suddenly the drums stopped. The chanting

stopped. The warriors stopped dancing. Elk Girl looked up and stifled a cry.

White Soldiers on large horses were riding into camp. They rode up to the circle of warriors. The White Soldier in the lead sat tall on his horse. He shouted words no one could understand. Then he pointed to Elk Girl crouching by the tree.

Elk Girl curled into a ball, trying to hide, but she peered through her fingers at the soldiers.

Long Nose stepped forward. "No take Ute girl," he said, shaking his head. He drew his knife.

The White Soldiers lifted their rifles.

Long Nose scowled and returned the knife to his side.

The tall White Soldier motioned with his arm, and a young soldier dismounted and walked toward Elk Girl. He spoke kindly to her, but she did not understand his words.

She did not resist when he cut the rope from her ankle and lifted her onto the horse behind the tall White Soldier. She had no strength left for caring.

The young soldier placed her arms around the tall White Soldier's waist and showed her how to hold on tight.

The sun was rising over the eastern mountains when the patrol crossed the Cache la Poudre River to Camp Collins. They stopped in front of a row of log cabins. The tall White Soldier dismounted, lifted Elk Girl down from the horse, and walked her to one of the cabins.

Elk Girl drew back in fear. This was a wooden tepee just as Magpie had said. She would never again see the blue sky. She would never again see the mountains. Fear swelled within her and she swayed against the rough logs.

"Mary," the tall White Soldier called.

The door opened and a woman appeared. She was small with hair the color of the sun. Her long dress was the color of the sun. This smiling woman, this golden sunflower, opened her arms wide and murmured soft words.

The woman was smiling. But then, Elk Girl remembered, Magpie had also smiled. She turned to run. But the tall White Soldier reached out and took her arm.

And led her inside the wooden tepee.

THREE

A Few Presents and an Indian Girl

1863

CHAPTER TEN

The White Woman called her Susan.

Elk Girl liked the way she said it so softly: Su-san, Su-san. But it was a White Woman's name. She was still Elk Tooth Dress. She nodded agreeably, however, and lay back on the cot the woman made up for her.

The next morning at the sound of the bugler's reveille, Elk Girl jumped up. "Ute," she said, pointing to herself. "Ute."

The White Soldier sat at the table, nodding his head. "Bill," he said, pointing to himself. "Sergeant Bill Carroll."

He pointed to the White Woman, who was bringing food to the table. "Mary."

The White Woman nodded. "Bill, Mary, Ute Susan."

Mary and Bill continued talking, making pictures with their hands. Elk Girl understood little of what they said, but she could see they were trying to please her and she nodded in agreement.

All morning Elk Girl watched Mary as she worked. Mary named whatever she did—washing dishes, making beds, drawing water from the well. Elk Girl tried to do whatever Mary did.

Later, skirting patches of spring snow, they walked down to the river. They sat on overturned buckets and watched the ducks.

"I am not a slave to the White Woman," Elk Girl whispered to the river. To the quacking ducks. To the sky. "I am not a slave." She smiled again and again. She brought her hands to her face to hide her joy, smiling still.

In the afternoon Mary opened a trunk at the foot of her bed and took out three folds of dress fabric. "Calico," she said, smoothing it with her hands.

Elk Girl nodded. She knew calico. She remembered that Quill Woman had wrapped a bolt of Turkey-red calico around her tepee, and the winter winds had blown it out across the prairie.

Mary pointed to each fold of fabric—one yellow, one blue, and one red. She pointed to her dress and then to Elk Girl.

Elk Girl stared in disbelief. The White Woman Mary wanted to make a dress for her. She pointed to Mary's dress and then to the yellow fabric. She wanted one just like Mary's.

"A yellow dress," Mary said.

And Elk Girl repeated, "A yel-low dress."

Mary took a paper pattern from the trunk and held it up to Elk Girl. Then she cut the dress, making it one size larger.

Two days later, the dress was finished. Mary slipped it over Elk Girl's head and helped her with the buttons.

She cut a narrow strip of the yellow fabric and tied it around Elk Girl's head, making a bow on top. Then she lifted out a looking glass from the trunk and leaned it against the wall. She motioned for Elk Girl to come and see.

Elk Girl gasped when she saw herself and covered her shorn head with her hands.

Mary took Elk Girl's hand and stood with her in front of the looking glass.

When Sergeant Bill opened the cabin door, they were still in front of the looking glass with their arms linked together. He pulled off his cap and ran his fingers through his bushy hair. "Beau-ti-ful," he exclaimed. "Beau-ti-ful."

In the days that followed, Elk Girl was content to help Mary with her daily chores. They cleaned the cabin, prepared meals, and planted a small vegetable garden behind the cabin. Often they walked to the river, dipping their toes into the swift, cold water. On the way back they picked yellow buttercups, and then arranged them in a glass jar for the kitchen table.

Each day Mary taught Elk Girl new words.

During the day they could hear Sergeant Bill in the background, shouting orders and drilling his men. One day Mary talked of Bill. He was a volunteer soldier for the state of Colorado, she said, because the regular soldiers were far away in the South fighting a civil war. Bill's cavalry protected a section of the Overland Trail, so people could travel in safety to California and Oregon.

Elk Girl strained to understand. She knew about California and Oregon. Quill Woman had told her about it. "Tell Bill"—she faltered for the words—"tell Bill—hurry to California-Oregon. The Cheyenne—kill soldiers—soon!"

Mary dropped the flowers she was gathering, took Elk Girl's hand, and hurried back to the cabin.

The days of the spring moon passed slowly. Elk Girl spent each day with Mary and Bill at the military fort. She felt safe.

Early one morning she was helping Mary

draw water from the well. Mary noticed a horse-drawn wagon pulling up to the sentry on the riverbank.

"It's Mr. Hollowell," she cried. "Come, Susan." She hurried over to the wagon. Elk Girl followed slowly.

The White Man sitting on the high wagon seat was singing, "'Tis the last rose of summer, left blooming alone . . ." When he saw Elk Girl, he stopped. Their eyes met.

Elk Girl gasped. He was the White Man who had come to the Arapaho camp. Long Nose had wanted to trade her—for the White Man's hat and looking glass. She trembled, remembering.

Mary exclaimed over the eggs and the fruit in the wagon. Then she looked up. "This is Susan," she said, reaching out. "The Ute girl. Susan, this is Mr. Hollowell."

The White Man nodded.

Elk Girl did not move. She stared at the White Man with the pale blue eyes. He had sent the White Soldiers. He had saved her from the Arapahos. Yet he was the real enemy. Mary and Bill were the real enemy.

She did not understand. She turned and hurried back to the cabin. Here in this cabin, wearing a yellow dress, she had almost forgotten she was Ute. She sat on her cot in silence.

The remainder of the day she was restless. She kept going to the cabin door, looking toward the mountains.

Mary tried to keep her occupied. She took out all the contents of her trunk—her wedding trousseau—and spread the articles on the bed. She told Elk Girl to choose another fabric for a new dress. And she used her engraved stationery to teach Elk Girl to write the new words she was learning to speak.

At first the slender pencil felt awkward to Elk Girl, and it slid from her hand. But she had stitched porcupine quills for Quill Woman, and she knew she could learn to write words for Mary Carroll. She set her hand to the paper.

Later they prepared supper for Bill—bacon and boiled cabbage and, for a treat, deviled eggs. They both waited anxiously for his arrival, and when he opened the door, Elk Girl rushed to meet him.

"I go—Bill. To Utes."

Bill glanced at Mary, who nodded. "She wants to go home, Bill. You must speak with Captain Hardy again."

Bill sighed, his hand still on the door latch. "I will speak to him again."

The answer was always the same. It was not a good time for a patrol to leave the fort. The Arapahos were hovering around the Overland Trail.

Bill tried to explain to Elk Girl. But she did not understand the ways of the White Soldiers. She understood only that she could not leave the wooden tepee.

Just as Magpie had said.

CHAPTER ELEVEN

The hot days of summer blended together, one after another, with little change until the day that the Carrolls called "the Glorious Fourth."

Elk Girl felt their anticipation of the day. Mary had made blue calico dresses and sunbonnets for both of them. And Mary had taught her many new words. Elk Girl liked to say "Glorious Fourth"; it made Mary smile.

For many days Sergeant Bill had assigned double fatigue duty to his men. He wanted the grounds and stables to be clean and orderly. The night before, he brushed and pressed his blue uniform and polished his black boots until he could see his reflection in them.

At the sound of the bugle on the awaited day, Elk Girl and Mary dressed in their new clothes and walked to the parade ground. The entire garrison had turned out, along with most of the citizens of the neighboring town of La Porte.

Elk Girl stood at Mary's side and watched as a red, white, and blue flag was slowly raised to the top of a pole. It was the same flag that the White Soldiers had carried as they marched across the prairie. She glanced sideways at Mary, then placed her hand over her heart as Mary did.

She thought, suddenly, of Quill Woman, who would like a bright calico flag waving from a tall pole. Then the Cheyenne would stand with their hands over their hearts in front of her beautiful tepee.

The cavalry performed drills, maneuvering their big horses through difficult formations. Elk Girl thought of her spotted pony with wings of the eagle on his shoulders and claws of the bear on his hooves. *Where was he now?* she wondered.

"Susan,"—Mary tugged on her sleeve— "just look at Bill. Doesn't he look grand on a horse?"

Elk Girl pushed back her sunbonnet to get a better look at Sergeant Bill on his large blood-bay horse. "Good Bill," she said.

After the formal activities, Sergeant Bill dismissed his men and walked around the grounds with his two "beau-ti-ful" girls. He nodded to the soldiers and the townspeople.

At noon, lunch was served outside the mess hall: roast pigs that had been sizzling over open fires since early dawn, baked beans, baking-powder biscuits, and ripe watermelons from Mr. Hollowell's garden.

After, Elk Girl walked with the Carrolls down to the riverbank where they sat in the shade of willow trees. In the afternoon they returned to the cabin so Bill could take a nap. He and Mary were looking forward to an evening of dancing and fireworks upriver at La Porte.

Inside the cabin Bill hung his dress coat and saber over a hook and pulled off his dusty boots. "Am I going to cut a caper tonight," he exclaimed, "with my two dancing girls!"

In his stockings he two-stepped with Mary around the cabin until she dropped into a chair. Then he offered his hand to Elk Girl. "May I have this dance, Miss Susan?"

Elk Girl fled to her cot. "Not—with White Man."

"Bill is not a White Man," he said, grinning. "Bill is Bill."

Elk Girl shook her head. "Not with White Man."

Bill withdrew his hand. "Another time," he said. "Tonight you may sit and listen to the fiddle and tap your feet. And watch the fireworks. Fire in the sky, Susan. You will like it."

Mary joined Elk Girl on her cot. "You do just what you want to," she said. "Go to the dance or stay at home. This is the Glorious Fourth of July, and we all want to be happy."

Elk Girl touched Mary's hand. "Su-san no dance. Su-san stay."

In the early evening Bill went to the stables to get his horse and wagon. Elk Girl waited with Mary at the cabin door.

"I will talk to Captain Hardy tonight," Mary said. "To remind him about the escort for you." When Bill arrived with the wagon, she gave Elk Girl a quick hug, then climbed up beside Bill. At the river bridge she turned and waved.

Elk Girl stood at the door waving until she could no longer see the wagon. Then she sat at the table and practiced her letters on Mary's stationery.

She occasionally glanced up at the window, and noticed the sky growing dark. It may have been the darkness that gave her the courage to leave. She did not know. She had not planned it.

Her heart beat rapidly as she pushed the paper aside. She moved about the cabin quickly before she changed her mind. She took her yellow dress, which was folded in the top of Mary's trunk, and a slab of ham from the cupboard. And a butcher knife. She rolled these into one of Mary's dish towels and tied it around her waist.

She hesitated at the door, knowing the

Carrolls would be worried when they returned to the empty cabin. Mary would weep. She went back to the table and sat down, undecided. She thought of Mary weeping and Bill trying to comfort her.

And then she thought of her home in the mountains. Her mother, Ouray, and Chipeta. It was summertime. They would be on the Uncompahgre mountain or at Middle Park for the horse races.

She ran her fingers across Mary's smooth, cream-colored paper, which still held Mary's sweet scent. She lifted her pencil and printed in large letters:

UTE SUSAN
THANK YOU

Elk Girl ran south on the Overland Trail, her footfalls soft in the hushed, moonlit night.

Suddenly from upriver she heard a roar of thunder. She stopped running and looked around, frightened. Fire shot into the sky. Then she remembered Bill's fireworks. He and Mary would be dancing together under the fiery sky. They would be happy.

And she was free. She raced quickly through the night.

At dawn, when the sky was flushed pink, she

found a cluster of bushes off to one side of the trail, and there she curled into a ball and slept.

Soon the warmth of the sun awakened her. She lay still, listening, clutching the butcher knife. Slowly she lifted her head and peered through the bushes.

A wagon rolled along the trail and several men on horseback passed by, their wide-brimmed hats hiding their faces.

She stayed hidden in the bushes, wondering if she should go out onto the trail in the daylight.

She saw another wagon approaching, drawn by a gray horse. The man on the wagon seat was singing a song—one she had heard before: "'Tis the last rose of summer, left blooming alone. . . ."

Mr. Hollowell.

She stepped out of the bushes and ran the short distance to the trail.

"Whoa." Mr. Hollowell pulled in the reins of his horse.

Elk Girl looked up shyly.

Mr. Hollowell removed his hat and hooked it over his knee. "Well, where did you come from, missy?"

Elk Girl pointed to the bushes.

"And where do you think you are going?"

"Over—mountains."

Mr. Hollowell peered ahead and then glanced over his shoulder. "Don't you know the Arapahos are looking for you?"

Elk Girl shook her head.

"In the middle of the night Sergeant Carroll rode over to their camp, thinking they had snatched you. At dawn six warriors rode up and down this trail, looking in every wagon. They poked through my load of cabbages. Spooked my horse."

Elk Girl shuddered. "Long Nose?"

"Yep. Don't know how he missed you in

that blue dress and bonnet." He slapped his dusty hat against his knee.

Elk Girl turned back toward the bushes.

"Wait," Mr. Hollowell called. "They will be coming back. Crawl in under my cabbages, missy. They have already poked through them. I am headed up the mountains to Central City, and you might as well come along too."

"Central City?"

"It's a boomtown," Mr. Hollowell said, "up high in the mountains. And it likes to think it's a regular town now. With new boardwalks on Main Street. And talk of a new hotel with real mattresses."

Mr. Hollowell glanced up the road. "Although hay beds are good enough for me. I prefer them, really. I sold them the hay." He looked back and coughed after his long monologue.

"I go with—cabbages," Elk Girl said quickly.

"Hop in," Mr. Hollowell said, nodding toward the back of the wagon. "When we get to Central City, you can just run on down the other side of the mountain and you'll be home. I'll tell the Carrolls where you went.

"I sure am talking today." He jumped down from the wagon and offered his knee. "Hop on up."

With Mr. Hollowell's help, Elk Girl wiggled herself down into the cabbages until she was hidden.

Mr. Hollowell climbed back up to the wagon seat and flicked the reins. "Giddyap, Rose," he called, and the horse set off at a brisk gait. Mr. Hollowell sang softly, "'Tis the last rose of the summer, left blooming alone. . . ."

The Arapahos soon returned, as Mr. Hollowell had said they would. Elk Girl heard the horses galloping toward them, snorting and puffing as they circled the wagon. She grasped her butcher knife, afraid the sound of her pounding heart would give her away.

Long Nose shouted. Mr. Hollowell stopped singing but continued on.

The warriors rode alongside the wagon for a while, yipping and taunting Mr. Hollowell. Then with a piercing cry from Long Nose, they galloped away. Elk Girl heard the sound of cabbages hitting the hard ground.

It seemed like a long time before Mr. Hollowell stopped the wagon. He sang the same song over and over again and exchanged greetings with other men on the trail. Had he forgotten her under the cabbages? She gasped for fresh air.

At last he lifted the cabbages that covered her. She looked into his kind eyes, and her heart filled with gratitude for this White Man.

She sat up. Then she reached up and kissed him on his cheek. Just as Mary would have done to Bill.

Mr. Hollowell turned pink. "Yep," he said, smiling. "Come and sit up front with me."

The trail was steep and narrow. At times Mr. Hollowell pulled off to the side of the road to let the faster wagons pass and to let his horse drink at the stream of water cascading down the mountainside.

"One of these trips," he said, "Rosie will turn into a golden mare just from drinking this water. There's solid gold under this creek."

Rose lifted her head from the stream and looked around at Mr. Hollowell. She switched her tail.

"But you can't eat it," Mr. Hollowell continued. "That's why I haul my cabbages up here. You can't eat it."

As they climbed slowly up the trail, other men on horseback passed them. They stared, and then rode ahead. One young man struck up a conversation.

"Name is Al Clements," he said. "Are you headed for Central City with those cabbages?"

"Yep," Mr. Hollowell said.

"And the girl?"

"I am giving her a ride up the mountain. She is going home to the Utes. I don't feel good dropping her off, though. Not in these mountains."

"My parents live in Central City," Clements said. "My father is the judge there. And my mother—she and her Methodist friends take in anybody. The girl will be in good hands."

Mr. Hollowell tipped his hat. "Much obliged," he said.

"Where do you think the Utes are now?" Clements asked. "I never see them in any of the mining towns. Never really see them at all anymore."

"Oh, I guess they stay clear of mining towns," Mr. Hollowell answered. "Guess they stay clear of *us* altogether. Probably back in the mountains somewhere."

"I don't suppose there are many Southerners still around either," Clements said.

"I don't suppose so. Nasty business, a civil war."

"And out west we have these cursed Indians . . ."

Elk Girl looked from Al Clements to Mr. Hollowell, bewildered. The White Men had another enemy?

They rode in silence for a while. At a narrow place in the road, Clements moved ahead. "If we lose contact," he called back, "meet me on Eureka Street in front of the law office."

Mr. Hollowell nodded.

As they climbed higher into the tall pines, Elk Girl trembled with excitement. If she'd had her own spotted pony, she would have leaped onto his back and ridden over the top of the mountains and down the other side. And raced into the waiting arms of her mother—

But she had no spotted pony. Only Mr. Hollowell's horse, walking slowly up the mountain trail. But she liked Mr. Hollowell and his old, gray Rose.

At the end of the day, when they were almost at the top of the mountains, they arrived at Central City. Treeless and scarred, the town had cabins and ore-crushing mills almost on top of one another that were clinging to the steep sides of gulches. Heavy ore wagons, each pulled by six horses, creaked up the dusty streets.

"Crazy boomtown," Mr. Hollowell said with a laugh. "A man spits out his front door and hits his neighbor's chimney."

He grinned at Elk Girl. "Let's go find this Mrs. Clements."

He leaned forward, looking for Eureka Street. "Stay at her house tonight, missy. I will stop by in the morning before I leave."

Mrs. Clements was a small woman like Mary, but older, and she carried herself with an air of importance. Her yellow-frame house on a steep side street was three times the size of Mary's cabin and was crowded with heavy furniture.

And she asked questions: "Was captivity dreadfully frightening for you, my dear? Whatever would you have done without kind Mr. Hollowell?"

She ushered Elk Girl up a steep stairway. "This is the guest bedroom," she explained, "and you are my guest." She pointed out the four-poster mahogany bed in the center of the room, the flowered Brussels carpet, and the lace curtains at the windows. She seemed very happy with her furniture.

At last Mrs. Clements stopped talking and closed the door behind her. Elk Girl lay down on the flowered carpet and, clutching the knife at her waist, fell asleep.

Downstairs in the parlor the next morning, Mrs. Clements spoke loudly and slowly to be certain that Elk Girl understood each word. "My husband, Judge Clements, has sent a dispatch to Governor Evans in Denver, who will certainly send a military escort to return you to your people. We all want good relations to prevail.

"Now," she said emphatically, "I do not know how to impress upon you that you must not go off on your own. Run away, I mean."

She heaved a deep sigh. "All men on this mountain are not good like Mr. Hollowell and my son. Some men are—"

"South-ern-ers?" Elk Girl had been saving the difficult word.

Mrs. Clements gasped and pulled a lace handkerchief from the neck of her dress and fanned herself vigorously. "Good gracious, girl. *Southerners*. What a thing to say. What do you know about our dreadful Civil War?"

From the parlor window Elk Girl saw Mr. Hollowell pull up in his wagon. She ran to greet him. Mrs. Clements followed behind, sputtering into her handkerchief.

"Now, my dear," she said, catching up, "stand modestly and say thank you to Mr. Hollowell, your friend and succor."

Elk Girl walked over to the wagon and

reached her arms up to Mr. Hollowell. Her eyes filled with tears and her voice trembled. "Thank you—Hollowell—White Man. Elk Girl not forget."

Mr. Hollowell leaned down and touched her hands. "Yep," he said shyly. Then he sat up, flicked the reins to Rose's back, and slowly pulled away.

Elk Girl waved until Mrs. Clements whispered to her, "That will do, my dear." She looked around anxiously. "Now I will call on my friends. We have much to do before the escort arrives. Come along."

Mrs. Clements walked up the front steps, paused, then turned back to Elk Girl. "And, my dear," she said with eyebrows raised, "must you really clutch that butcher knife so?"

CHAPTER THIRTEEN

On her fifth day at the Clements's house, Elk Girl peered through the window of the guest bedroom to the street below and saw two horsemen riding up the narrow street, leading two packhorses and a bay pony. They stopped at the Clements's picket gate.

A White Man dismounted, whirled his reins around the gatepost, and walked up the steps to the front door. The other man, dressed in buckskin, waited on his black horse. A wide-brimmed hat hid his face, and thick, dark braids fell over his shoulders. Could it be Ouray who had come for her?

Elk Girl leaned forward, moving the lace curtain, and the young man looked up. Quickly she drew back, disappointed. He was a White Man.

Elk Girl collected her belongings—the two calico dresses and the butcher knife— and walked from the bedroom. She paused in front of a looking glass in the hall to see herself in the clothing Mrs. Clements had provided.

Mrs. Clements had insisted that Elk Girl's calico dresses were not suitable for a journey on horseback. She and her friends had outfitted her in appropriate western dress—a wool gaberdine divided skirt and a long-sleeved jacket, knee-high leather boots, leather gloves, and a wide-brimmed hat to protect her from the sun and hide her short hair.

Elk Girl stared at herself in disbelief.

From the top of the stairs she watched as Judge Clements answered the knock at the front door. Then quickly she moved to the halfway landing to listen to the men talk.

"Agent Simeon Whiteley," the man said, offering his hand. "I have been sent by Governor Evans for the Ute girl." He removed his hat as he stepped inside.

"You are the military escort?" Judge Clements asked.

"I am the escort," Whiteley said, slapping the gun on his hip. "With my interpreter, Uriah Curtis." He nodded toward the street. "He speaks Ute just like an Indian."

He moved closer to the judge and talked faster. "This is not a military move, you realize. You could call it political. We want the Ute chiefs to come to the Conejos Agency on October first for a treaty."

Elk Girl leaned forward, straining to understand. She knew "treaty." Ouray had told her to talk treaty.

"And returning the girl will persuade them of your sincerity?" the judge asked.

"She is the sister of Chief Ouray!" Whiteley exclaimed. He shrugged his shoulders. "It's worth a try."

"And you expect to find them in Middle Park?"

"That's right. Around Sulphur Springs. The Ute bands meet there every summer to race their horses. So that's where the new agency will be built for distribution of their supplies and rations. And presents, of course."

"For signing away their land on October first," the judge said quietly.

"W-well," Whiteley stuttered. He lifted his hands in exasperation. "Sir, I am here to help them," he said. "Give them food. I'm on their side."

"I'll call Mrs. Clements and the girl," the judge said.

Outside, Elk Girl stood by the picket gate with the Clements.

"Tell her the pony is hers," Whiteley said to Uriah Curtis. "A gift from the Great White Father." He gave Elk Girl a boost onto the back of the bay pony.

Elk Girl settled into the saddle and rubbed her hand against the warm neck of the mare. She was surprised that Curtis had spoken to her in her own language. She wondered about this man who spoke Ute and wore buckskin. And who was the Great White Father?

As the small procession turned down Eureka Street, Elk Girl looked back and waved to Mrs. Clements and the judge standing at their gate. Mrs. Clements waved a lace handkerchief.

Dogs barked and snapped at the horses as they moved down the narrow street. Merchants came to their doors to watch, and miners looked up from their ore wagons.

Elk Girl felt she would burst with happiness. She was going home. These two White Men would ride with her to Middle Park to protect her from Long Nose and his warriors. The Utes would be surprised to see her riding in with two White Men. They would see that the White Men were not the real enemy, after all.

They followed Clear Creek and passed through mining camps clinging to the side of the mountains—Idaho Springs and Empire.

They climbed through pale, quaking aspens, trembling in the breeze, and through dark pines. They climbed higher than the trees, and at the end of the day they stopped on top of the windswept mountains.

Whiteley waved his hat. "We are on top of the Continental Divide," he exclaimed. "On top of the world." He looked around. "Tell the girl, Curtis."

"She knows," Curtis said.

The wind whipped against them as they made a hasty camp and crawled into their bedrolls. Elk Girl lay quietly, watching the silver stars spread across the dark sky, too happy to sleep.

"We should start seeing Utes any time now," Whiteley said the next morning as they saddled their horses. "We are on their side of the mountains. You take the lead, Curtis. You speak Indian." He laughed. "Heck, Curtis, you even look like one."

Elk Girl watched the two men, so different from each other. Whiteley was stout and talked much of the time. Curtis was tall and thin. And quiet. They both seemed uneasy with her, yet they were kind.

As they moved down the mountain, Whiteley shouted ahead to Curtis. "If you really can speak two languages, Curtis, I wish you would prove it to me. Just talk, Curtis!"

Curtis reined in his horse and turned in his saddle. "A rider is following us. He has been trying to catch up to us all morning."

"A Ute?" Whiteley strained his neck, looking back up the trail.

Curtis motioned for them to move from the trail. "This is the first stand of trees we've passed this morning," he said. "We can wait for him here. And he is not Ute."

"You see him now?" Whiteley said, still scanning the trail behind.

"He'll be coming over that ridge behind us—soon," Curtis said. "Move into the trees."

Minutes later Curtis moved out from the

trees and startled a young cavalryman. As his horse reared, the young man clung to the saddle horn. "Thought you were an Indian," he shouted.

He carried a dispatch from Governor Evans with word of a Ute outbreak in Wyoming near Fort Halleck, just north of Middle Park. He advised Whiteley to move with caution into Middle Park and to wait there for a military escort.

His message delivered, the cavalryman looked around quickly, then rode back up the trail.

Curtis, Whiteley, and Elk Girl moved on down the trail. At the top of each ridge they stopped to scan the broad valley. There was no sign of Ute camps.

Elk Girl shifted uneasily in her saddle. She had heard the message, but what did it mean? Where were her people?

Whiteley stood in his stirrups and looked

around. "Where are those sons of guns, Curtis? You think the entire Ute nation is up fighting at Fort Halleck?"

"Perhaps a few are up there fighting encroachment," Curtis said. "The others are back in the mountains, I imagine, not knowing what to do."

"They are supposed to come to Sulphur Springs. That's what they're supposed to do," Whiteley said. "And when they come,"—he shook his fist—"they had better come peacefully. I am not prepared to fight them. Just feed them and get them to Conejos to sign."

Curtis sighed. "They will be what you call 'peaceful,'" he said. "They can hardly come any other way, scattered as they are. And beaten down by poverty and smallpox."

Elk Girl reined in her pony and stared at Curtis. Surely he was talking about the Cheyenne and the Arapahos. They were the ones who were beaten down by the

White Men. Not the People of the Shining Mountains. Not the Utes.

Both men noticed her agitation and reined in their horses. "Do you think she is tired?" Whiteley asked, looking at Curtis.

Curtis nodded. "I think so."

"Do you think she understands English?"

"She—understands," Elk Girl said, her voice low but clear.

The men looked at each other, surprised.

"Let's make camp," Curtis said.

CHAPTER FOURTEEN

In Middle Park they camped in a grove of quaking aspens near the hot springs to wait for the military escort.

Whiteley and Curtis jumped into the hot pools in their long johns. "Come on in," Whiteley called to Elk Girl. "The water is on fire." They hopped up and down and beat their fists against their chests. And hollered.

Elk Girl shook her head. But she watched the antics of the men out of the corner of her eye as she rubbed down her mare. Later she turned the pony loose to graze, and she gathered firewood. When her arms were loaded, the men leaped from the pools and took the wood from her. They would do the men's work, they said.

After that, Elk Girl picked berries and brought them back to camp in her felt hat. The men were pleased with that.

And she raced her pony through the tall, waving grass. The valley was deserted, with no signs of anyone having camped there that summer. The vast silence was unsettling to Elk Girl.

After several days Curtis became restless and joined her on a pony ride. They raced across the valley and up into the foothills. Elk Girl liked Curtis racing by her side. He was quick, and nothing missed his eye. He was like a fox.

They returned to camp at dusk and found Whiteley had climbed a tall tree to scan the mountain trail. "How long can it take for a wagon to move over a mountain?" he called. "It's the middle of July."

Whiteley was still agitated as they sat around the campfire eating a rabbit that Curtis had shot. "And where are those Utes? How will they ever learn to farm if they don't stay in one place?"

Curtis raked the ashes with a stick. "You know it is not the nature of Indians to stay in one place. They are hunters, not farmers."

"You're a White Indian, Curtis," Whiteley shouted. "Why don't they stay in one place?"

"I just told you the reason," Curtis said. "It's not their nature."

"Well, I feel like a sitting duck here," Whiteley said.

The days passed slowly and quietly. Whiteley walked around with the agency plans rolled under his arm, stepping off distances and pounding in stakes. "Stand there in the corner," he called to Elk Girl. And he called, "Walk this off, Curtis."

Curtis hunted small game, and Elk Girl picked berries. In the evenings all three soaked in the hot pools—the men in their long johns and Elk Girl in her yellow dress.

Elk Girl remembered bobbing in the pools with Chipeta, listening to the stories of old Skunk Eyes. She remembered the old woman telling her of someone left on the prairie with a broken leg. It seemed a long time ago.

Whiteley stayed in the pools for only a short time, and then cooled off on the smooth rocks. "You two Indians are going to melt away in there," he shouted.

Elk Girl and Curtis soaked in the water, talking sometimes in Ute, sometimes in English. At times they spoke with their hands.

Elk Girl told Curtis about her past two years, years that seemed like a lifetime. She talked of Twisted Hair and Quill Woman. The yellow dog. Long Nose and Magpie. She talked of the Carrolls and Mr. Hollowell and Mrs. Clements. "I would like to be like Mary Carroll," she said shyly.

"I walked here from Missouri," Curtis told her, "after my folks died. It was a long walk. I passed the camps of the Plains Indians and the herds of buffalo. I walked until I bumped into the Shining Mountains, and then I stopped."

"And now you will stay?" Elk Girl asked.

"The mountains are my home now. I will stay."

Elk Girl moved closer to him. "You will be happy here with us in the Shining Mountains. Safe and happy with the Utes."

Curtis took her hand in his. "Elk Girl, I need to tell you something. You saw how the

Cheyenne and the Arapahos are beaten down? How they no longer hunt the buffalo? How they line up for food and blankets?"

Elk Girl nodded. "That happened on the prairie."

Curtis looked into Elk Girl's eyes as he spoke. "It grieves me to tell you this, but do you know who Simeon Whiteley is? He is an agent for the United States government. He is here to build an agency to hand out food and blankets to the Utes, here in Middle Park. The Shining Mountains have been penetrated by the White Men."

Elk Girl withdrew her hand and stared at Curtis. She could not believe what he said.

"Your brother Ouray is trying to save your people by keeping the peace. He signs treaties. He has signed away much of the Shining Mountains already. Still the White Men keep coming, Elk Girl. They have already won."

Elk Girl covered her face with her hands and wept silently.

Curtis put his arms around her trembling shoulders, trying to comfort her. "The Utes will survive," he said, "but only within boundaries. I urge you to tell your people not to keep fighting the White Men. Because," he whispered, "there is no hope."

Gray steam encircled Elk Girl and Curtis, hiding them. Whiteley called out to them from the rocks. "Hey, where are you two Indians?"

Day after day, Whiteley climbed the tall tree, scanning the mountain trail. Then he walked around his outlined agency. Each day he shook his head and muttered, "It seems we have everything for an agency except supplies. And Indians."

One morning he decided to abandon his building plans.

"Curtis," he said, "continue on with the girl until you run into Indians. Any band will do. Bribe them, Curtis, with beads and the girl. Whatever it takes to get them to Conejos by October first so they can sign the treaty."

Elk Girl looked from Whiteley to Curtis, confused.

"And young man,"—Whiteley placed his hand on Curtis's shoulder—"don't get sweet on the girl. That's an order."

Whiteley swung into his saddle and headed for the trail. "And when those cursed Indians get hungry," he shouted, "they can come begging at Empire on the White side of the mountains. That's where I will be!"

Elk Girl and Curtis rode west, following Ute trails. They wound their way through the tall mountains and then dropped down to the Grand River. They followed the river, hoping to find an encampment of Tabeguache.

They rode late each night until they could no longer see the trail. Then they lay down under shaggy juniper trees until daybreak.

Days later they reached the vast wall of the Uncompahgre Plateau. Elk Girl became excited. Her people would be on the mountain, she told Curtis. Only the Tabeguache Utes camped on this high mountain with the craggy slopes. She and Curtis began the steep ascent up the north end.

The climb up the jagged mountain was difficult and slow, and when they reached the crest, they camped for the night. At daybreak they set out again, circling massive rock formations and patches of dense pines, looking for the trail that ran the length of the mountain. At dusk they left the rocky terrain and moved down into a meadow. There they found the trail.

The next day, as they circled more rocks and boulders, they saw below a small lake and, scattered around it, Ute tepees.

Elk Girl caught her breath and reined in her pony. A great longing surged within her as she looked down at the camp. These were her people—her mother, Ouray, and Chipeta. She was home at last. She turned to Curtis riding behind her.

She could not leave Curtis. He had watched over her for half the summer. He had brought food and water and each night made a soft bed for her. And he had brought joy to her heart.

She spoke hesitantly. "Curtis is a good White Man. Not real enemy."

Curtis moved swiftly to her side and touched her shoulder. "I am a White Indian," he said.

"Elk Girl—White Indian too," Elk Girl said, smiling. And having difficulty saying what she felt, she crossed her arms and pressed them to her heart.

Curtis crossed his arms over his heart. "You are in my heart too, Elk Girl," he said. "But soon"—he sighed—"I must report back to Simeon Whiteley, who will report to the President of the United States—the Great White Father."

He reached over and took her hands in his. "I will never be far away."

They rode into camp strangely unnoticed, moving around tepees that were shabby and faded. Men sat around small fires, eating and tossing bones to groveling dogs. Occasionally someone looked up.

Elk Girl stared in disbelief. These were the Tabeguache, her people. But something was wrong. Her people looked like the Cheyenne and Arapahos—wrapped in blankets of the White Men.

She looked at Curtis, and he nodded sadly.

An old man wrapped in a blanket rose slowly and walked over to them. A scrawny dog jumped for a piece of meat in his hand.

"Greetings," Curtis said. "Will you point the way to Chief Ouray?"

The old man tossed the meat to the dog and drew the blanket closer to his thin body. He pointed to a tepee set apart from the others.

Curtis nudged his pony forward. Elk Girl rode slowly behind.

Elk Girl saw her brother step from his tepee. He stood big and broad and proud with his arms folded across his chest. His eyes were focused on Curtis.

"Greetings, Chief Ouray," Curtis said in Ute. "I come on an errand from Agent Simeon Whiteley for the United States government."

He reached for a leather pouch behind his saddle, fumbling as he untied it. "I bring presents and"—he turned and extended his arm to Elk Girl—"and"—his voice wavered—"a Ute girl."

CHAPTER FIFTEEN

"Elk Tooth Dress, my sister!" Ouray exclaimed.

Hearing Ouray's voice, Chipeta stepped out from her tepee, and Bird Track from hers. Little Paron, playing nearby, ran to his father's side.

Elk Girl slid from her pony and looked from one to another—Ouray, Chipeta, Paron, and her mother. She wanted to shout with joy, but no sound came. Tears filled her eyes.

They stared at her—at her riding suit, at her leather boots, at her wide-brimmed hat.

They stared at the White Man in buckskin with long dark braids.

"I have come home." Elk Girl's voice trembled. "The White Soldiers rescued me from the Arapahos. And Curtis"—she motioned to him—"brought me here."

She touched her woolen jacket and divided skirt. "White Woman's clothes," she said. She slipped her hat from her head, revealing her short, scraggly hair.

Bird Track gasped and raised her hands to her head.

Ouray stepped forward and took Elk Girl's hands in his. "We thank the Great Spirit for your return, little sister," he said. "We will dance. We will sing."

He reached out his hand to Curtis, still sitting on his horse. "Chief Ouray, chief of all Utes, gives thanks to Curtis for returning his sister. Stay awhile with us."

As the sun slid down the red sky behind the mountain, the old men squatted near the campfire with drums between their knees. *Tap, tap, tap,* the drums sounded. Soft and low.

The Tabeguache heard the drums and gathered around the campfire. When the sky darkened and the fire blazed bright, they began dancing.

The women danced first. They formed a single line, hopping on one leg, limping on the other, around and around the leaping fire. The drummers sang and beat their drums louder.

The men joined in, reaching for a partner from the swaying line of women. They danced side by side, stepping forward, stepping back. Singing softly.

Elk Girl walked shyly over to Curtis, who was standing alone, and drew him into the circle of dancers. She placed her right arm around his waist. Hesitantly, he placed his left arm around her waist.

They danced together, stepping forward, stepping back, around the campfire. But Curtis did not have dancing feet, he said. He grinned and moved back to the shadows alone.

The Utes danced under a pale moon long into the night, until the old men stopped drumming and singing, and the fire fluttered low. Then the dancers drifted silently to their tepees.

Bird Track's bones ached.

Early each morning Elk Girl helped her walk outside to greet the rising sun. Then Bird Track reclined in a willow backrest while Elk Girl combed her hair with a porcupine-tail comb. Bird Track had thin, gray hair like Quill Woman's, she noticed.

"I gave up hope," Bird Track said, reaching up to touch Elk Girl's hand. "Ouray made many trips to the prairie to spy on the Arapahos."

"I was with the Cheyenne at first," Elk Girl said. Her voice was sad as she remembered. "They were always moving away from the White Men."

"As we do now," Bird Track said.

They looked up as two hunters rode into camp.

"Again our young men return with no deer," Bird Track said. "Only jackrabbits. The White Men have chased the black-tailed deer off Mother Earth, as they did the buffalo."

She sighed wearily. "When the snow falls, we will go down to the Gunnison River—to the White Men's agency. Bad food. Bad blankets." She spit on the ground.

"I know," Elk Girl whispered. "But I am here to help now. And the Great Spirit knows of us."

Curtis spent the last days of summer with the Utes. And, too soon, the day came when he said, "It is time for me to go."

He and Ouray had returned from an early-morning hunt with jackrabbits hanging across the backs of their ponies. They dropped the game in front of Bird Track's tepee.

"We will ride with you, Curtis," Ouray said. "Elk Tooth Dress and I—to the fork in the trail."

Elk Girl mounted her bay pony and rode out of camp with the men. They followed the worn trail across green meadows, through dense pines and quaking aspens, and along thickets of tall chokecherry bushes heavy with red berries. Ouray reached out and broke off a slender branch of chokecherry.

At a large boulder marking the fork in the trail, they reined in their ponies. They looked down at the Gunnison River Valley far below—the pale curving river, the grassland scattered with log cabins.

Ouray pointed out the trail winding down the mountain, partly hidden by foliage and rocks. Then he lifted the chokecherry branch into the air and held it out to Curtis.

"Peace," he said.

"Peace to you, Chief Ouray," Curtis said as he accepted the branch. Then he asked, "Chief Ouray, what shall I tell Simeon Whiteley?"

Ouray sat tall on his black mare. "Tell Simeon Whiteley"—he looked at Elk Girl— "tell him we will go to Conejos—to save our people. We will talk treaty."

Curtis nodded.

"The fighting words," Elk Girl said softly.

She knew, even now, that the White Men had won the fight. They had already built their fences in the Shining Mountains.

Curtis knew.

Ouray knew.

She looked at her brother. Ouray, broad of shoulders and strong. Sober and cool-headed. He had known since he was a boy in Taos what would happen. Now he was tired of talking, tired of signing treaties.

He turned his pony back toward camp.

Curtis rode a short distance down the steep trail. Then he looked back, lifted the peace branch, and galloped away.

For a long while Elk Girl sat looking after Curtis, even though she could no longer see him on the trail. Her pony tossed his head, snorting and blowing.

"Good-bye," she whispered. "I will not forget." She turned her pony slowly toward home.

The tall pines whispered as she passed, and the aspens trembled and sighed. Berries of the chokecherry fell to the ground like raindrops. Then from a distance came the faint sound of hand drums: *tap, tap, tap*.

Elk Girl reined in her pony. Drums were beating. Drums were calling her.

She dropped low over the pony's back and pressed her knees into his belly. "Go, little bay," she whispered. "Go like the wind."

The Utes were dancing.

Cutshutchous, or Elk Tooth Dress

Elk Girl played a valiant part in the history of the American West during the latter part of the nineteenth century.

She was known by several names. Her Ute name was *Cutshutchous,* which means "Elk Tooth Dress." It was customary for Utes to have more than one name during their lives, and abbreviations were commonly used. The name Susan was given to her by Mary Carroll, and it is generally the name historians use to identify her.

Major events in her life have been recorded and, surprisingly, so have numerous details about her experiences, such as the dresses made for her by Mary Carroll and her wagon ride under the cabbages.

Elk Girl was a Tabeguache Ute. She was born in 1845, high in the Rocky Mountains of Colorado. Her people had lived for centuries isolated and protected from the outside world by the mountain wall.

But she was born to a time of change. In 1858 gold was discovered along Cherry Creek in the eastern foothills near present-day Denver, and the White encroachment began.

Her life was also tragically changed when she was kidnapped as a young girl by marauding Indians from the Plains. Her rescue from the Arapahos two years later by a White farmer and United States soldiers from Camp Collins is irony, indeed.

Elk Girl reentered history, as Susan Johnson, when she was thirty-four years old at the time of the Ute uprising known as the

Meeker Massacre of September 29, 1879. She lived with her Ute husband, known as Johnson, and two sons at the White River Agency. She lived in a log cabin, as Chief Ouray did at the Los Pinos Agency. Both tried to set a good example for the Ute people.

Nathan Meeker arrived at the White River Agency in the spring of 1878. He was determined to "civilize" the Utes; he would turn them into farmers. The Utes did not cooperate. When Meeker began plowing a favorite horse-racing pasture, they revolted.

The Utes ambushed a military troop sent to aid Meeker, and then killed Meeker and all his employees. They took three women and two children captive and fled to the top of Grand Mesa, a flat-topped mountain high above the Grand River.

Elk Girl rode her horse to the mountain hideout and tried to help with negotiations. One thousand United States soldiers were marching toward the mountain, and the Ute warriors threatened to kill the captives if the soldiers continued.

Acting on the authority that she was Chief Ouray's sister, Elk Girl demanded that the warriors release the captives to her. The warriors did so, sullenly, perhaps out of fear of Chief Ouray or because the soldiers were advancing rapidly toward the mountain.

The troops were stopped and the captives were taken to Chief Ouray's home.

The Meeker women, in interviews, lectures, and correspondence, always gave thanks and credit to Elk Girl for saving their lives. Elk Girl had not forgotten a time long ago. She repaid the debt.

As a result of the Meeker Massacre, the White River Utes and the Tabeguache Utes were driven from their majestic mountain homes to a desolate reservation in eastern Utah.

Elk Girl lived the remainder of her life on

the Uintah-Ouray Reservation. She died in the early spring, at the time of the Bear Dance on March 5, 1901, at the age of fifty-six.

The name of the Tabeguache was changed to Uncompahgre, after the agency that was established for them in the Uncompahgre River Valley in 1875. They, however, continue to call themselves Tabeguache.

Still today, each spring on the Uintah-Ouray Reservation, the Ute people dance their traditional Bear Dance as Elk Girl once did.

Margaret K. McElderry Books • An imprint of Simon & Schuster Children's
Publishing Division • 1230 Avenue of the Americas, New York, New York 10020

Text copyright © 2005 by Thelma Hatch Wyss • Map copyright © 2005 by Derek Grinnell
All rights reserved, including the right of reproduction in whole or in part in any form.
Book design by Sonia Chaghatzbanian • The text for this book is set in Adobe
Caslon. • Manufactured in the United States of America • 10 9 8 7 6 5 4 3 2 1
Library of Congress Cataloging-in-Publication Data • Wyss, Thelma Hatch. • Bear
Dancer : the story of a Ute girl / Thelma Hatch Wyss.—1st ed. • p. cm. • Summary:
In late-nineteenth-century Colorado, Elk Dress Girl, sister of Ute chief Ouray, is cap-
tured by Cheyenne and Arapaho warriors, rescued by the white "enemy," and finally
returned to her home. Includes historical notes. • ISBN-13: 978-1-4169-0285-0
ISBN-10: 1-4169-0285-6 1. Tabeguache Indians—Juvenile fiction. 2. Ute Indians—
Juvenile fiction. [1. Tabeguache Indians—Fiction. 2. Ute Indians—Fiction.
3. Indians of North America—Colorado—Fiction. 4. Ouray—Fiction.]
I. Title. PZ7.W998Bea 2005 • [Fic]—dc22 • 2005040620

FIRST
V
EDITION